LOVE IN BETWEEN

A BELLETHORPE NOVELLA

LEANNE LOVEGROVE

LOVE IN BETWEEN

Love in Between by **Leanne Lovegrove**

Finding community, and love, in the most unexpected place.

Caleb Stirling has never had it easy, but he's worked hard and is a stellar chef of his own five-star restaurant in Sydney. Over one fateful week his world crumbles around him and he finds himself in an outback country town where everything he's ever known is threatened.

Bridie Finch is the lifeblood of *Bellethorpe*. Need something done? Give it to Bridie. She's so busy looking after the community, her father and their strawberry farm, she fails to care for herself.

Now, Caleb must care for his orphaned niece. But Bridie needs a chef for the annual Bastille Day Festival and, unwillingly, he lands the role. But there's no place to hide in town and soon the locals discover who he really is. Instead of rejecting him, they rally with support and quickly both Bellethorpe and Bridie get under his skin.

A sweet small-town story of community, being accepted and finding love in the most unexpected of places.

LOVE IN BETWEEN

LEANNE LOVEGROVE

This story was always dedicated to Sue, my friend, a fellow writer. But quite ironically, in a cruel twist of fate, since I wrote this novella, we lost her unexpectedly and too soon. This book is dedicated to her and our friendship.

Leanne Lovegrove

1

Caleb Stirling watched the whirlybird of dust spiral past and thought he must have arrived on the set of a crime show. The squeaking school gate, swinging to and fro, added to the effect.

A cascade of goosebumps erupted across his skin.

Inside the gate, the head mistress of Bellethorpe Primary School, whom he'd successfully avoided the last three mornings in a row, frowned in his direction. Her gaze so intent that he felt trapped like fruit in jelly.

If he avoided her eye, could he slink past unscathed? He'd try.

Taking great interest in Sybella walking beside him, he reached for her tiny hand. In a traitorous move, she dodged his touch and raced away to her friends gathered near the adventure playground. The children's mothers nattered to each other and stared at him too, just like every other day. In time he'd talk to them, but not today. A presence stepped beside him and his heart sank. His luck had run out. He'd avoided contact with anyone at the school, hell, the entire town since he'd arrived in the backwater that was Bellethorpe. Not for the first time he wondered why his sister had lived in the small country town, which on first glance, had little to offer. And in the midst of winter, it was bloody cold.

'Sybella says she hasn't eaten breakfast these last few mornings,' Mrs Ackhurst addressed him. She leaned in as she spoke and then recoiled with her nose in the air. For some reason, he expected her to have grey, permed hair and a chain with glasses around her neck. Prim and proper and sensibly dressed, yes, but she wasn't as old as he'd imagine. Her voice was stern though, and she clasped her hands together as she waited for his reply to a question she hadn't asked.

He thought for a moment trying to remember. He'd seen the kid eat, hadn't he?

'Nor has she had any lunch,' Mrs Ackhurst continued.

'You don't provide lunch?' he enquired.

'There's a tuckshop, Mr Stirling, but she needs money to purchase food.'

Caleb felt his pockets and blew out a sigh of relief as he extracted a couple of gold coins.

'And you need to pre-order.'

Ah. He fondled the coins in his hand.

'Let me escort you. And, on this occasion only, we'll accept a late order. Orders must be in by midday the day before.'

She couldn't be serious. He glanced across at Sybella; each time he looked at the diminutive fragile girl, his heart melted into a pool in his hollow chest. Those black curls, dark eyes; it was like looking at his sister. Sybella sat with a grim expression while her friends laughed and chatted. They were like clones in the identical uniform except their hair was tied into two plaits that ran the length of their tiny backs, their school dresses uncreased and their black shoes, polished. Sybella wore runners with the laces undone and carried a light-weight backpack. It was pink with unicorns on it. The other girls had similar bags but theirs bulged with drink bottles and books.

Darn, Mrs Ackhurst drew him back to the present. Couldn't she let it rest? 'This way, Mr Stirling,' and like the children she taught, Caleb obeyed and followed behind as she strode ahead. She said good morning to each child she passed and their parents. Caleb pulled his cap down lower and hands in his pockets, focused on his shoes

It was only a short walk to the canteen where a bright red sign welcomed you to *Bite Right Inn*. He cringed.

'Oh, thank goodness, Mrs Ackhurst. Mrs Bingham hasn't arrived, and the food preparation isn't complete...'

Mrs Ackhurst held up her flat palm. 'Calm down, Kathleen.'

Kathleen took a deep breath and wiped her hands down her black apron.

'I have the perfect solution. Mr Stirling,' she turned and pointed at him, 'is a chef new to the community. He'll help out, won't you, Mr Stirling?'

What? Uh ah, she had the wrong culprit. He glanced at the basic stainless-steel kitchen with two women hovering near benchtops, knives and other utensils in their hands.

'Don't you simply heat up sausage rolls and make hot dogs and give out lolly bags?'

His words were steady, but his heart hammered fast and his throat constricted. He now regretted that bottle of whiskey last night.

Kathleen smirked and the head teacher replied. 'Perhaps when you were at school, Mr Stirling, but today, it's all about Smart Choices and healthy eating and drinking.'

Kathleen bounced on her toes and jumped in. 'There're categories, you see, there's a poster on the wall over there explaining the details. The top and most important is the green category which is foods you can enjoy in abundance. The amber category is food to select *very* carefully and the red, well, is occasional only.'

What the hell? Someone was pulling his leg.

A nearby door slammed and brought with it a gust of wind down the narrow corridor. Heels clacked on the linoleum floor and broke the silence. The women on both sides of him broke into broad smiles.

He followed their gazes and watched another lady approach. Where were all the men in this town? This woman was different to others he'd met so far. She wore pink heeled boots compared to Mrs Ackhurst's sensible brogues in a muted camel colour. Dark blue jeans matched a bright pink collared tee which featured a large, ripe strawberry on her left breast. She was well-groomed with make-up and long, luscious mahogany locks that curled in slight waves and sat in perfect strands on each side of her face, coming to rest below her shoulders

'Good morning Bridie,' Mrs Ackhurst greeted her. 'How are you today?'

'Fabulous, thank you, Roberta. Hi Kathleen,' she matched their beaming welcome. She paused and stared at him, her smile faltering. He was getting lots of that, too. Were the rumours about small towns true? She threw a quick peek at the two women before asking, 'Is everything all right?' Her smile dropped and her eyes scanned him, starting at his shoes and moving at a leisurely pace until it stalled on his right arm. Most people did that, too. The length of his right arm, commencing at the wrist up to pretty much his shoulder, was covered in art. Black ink.

Caleb removed his cap and ran his hands through his hair and dragged them across his stubble-covered cheeks. God, he must look a sight. He'd been wearing these clothes for days and had slept in them too. At least the black jeans didn't crease but his ratty t-shirt with the portrait of some singer he couldn't even name, hadn't faired so well.

An obnoxious chorus of music blared out through invisible speakers, jolting his thoughts. Mrs Ackhurst let it finish before speaking again. 'That's the start of the school day. I must be off. Mr Stirling, as I was saying, it would be of great help to the school if you could provide some assistance today. It won't take long. We're short and the children need to eat.'

Did she think he was some Jamie Oliver celebrity chef cooking up school dinners? 'I'm sorry that isn't possible. Can she do it?' He pointed at the beautiful brunette, Bridie they said. It was a low act, he knew.

'Are you short, Kathleen? Where's Polly?'

'I don't know, but she's not here and we aren't to expect her.'

As Bridie listened, she was already removing her coat and nodding agreement, her beautiful crystal-clear eyes, contemplative. No doubt her mind was whirring, too. 'I have my own disaster this morning. The chef I use every year for the Bastille Day Festival has pulled out and I need to find another one, pronto. It's only a month away, so I have to get that organised. But of course, that can wait until later. I'll help this morning. We can't let the children starve.'

Mrs Ackhurst observed him again. 'Well, this is timely, Bridie. This is Caleb Stirling, new to town and Sybella's... um... Yes, well, he's a city chef just arrived in Bellethorpe who's sure to help with the festival.'

This time he quickly raised his hand as if that would quell the conversation, but the women ignored him and disbursed. Bridie gripped his wrist, 'C'mon, I'll show you the ropes and we'll get this done in no time. We can chat about the festival too.'

He glanced at his wrist in her grasp. Her fingernails were short but flamingo pink. This woman was a pink powderpuff, all feminine and light and pretty. She was enticing him in all sorts of ways, and his body stirred at the sight of her, but really, all he wanted was to sink back onto the couch and sleep the next few hours away. Forget for a little longer.

Instead, he followed suit, doing what he was told for the second time this morning. In the kitchen she handed him an apron and he robotically placed it over his head and tied the knot at the back; something he'd done a thousand times before. But not since... not in this kitchen either.

'I'm not cooking,' he said, his words harsh and lost on Bridie who was busy gathering lettuces from the fridge and placing them on the bench in front of him. Someone lit the gas stovetop and he jumped at the ignition sound. Bridie paused, her hand on the bench next to his fisted knuckle. Her chest inflated with an intake of breath and her eyes squinted. She moved away to rummage in her handbag before extracting a box. She grabbed a glass of water and collected an apple from the fruit bowl. Without saying a word, she popped out two tiny white tablets, placed them in her palm, waited until he took them and he'd swallowed with a large gulp. When he was finished, she handed him the apple.

How did she know?

2

Well, what a surprise; that wasn't how she'd expected her morning to proceed, it had been a little exciting. First the disaster at school; how could she not pitch in? It had been a rush of prepping salad rolls and fruit cups and baking banana and choc chip muffins. She made a mental note to check on Polly. She might need a homemade lasagne.

Then there was the setback for the festival but what a relief there was a newcomer in town. He'd help. How had she not met him already? He'd been here three whole days. Perhaps they should organise a welcome dinner? Given he's a chef that might not work. A cocktail night or wine tasting at one of their prestigious vineyards? Bridie was sure he'd fall in love with their local produce. Bridie remembered his arm of tattoos and shivered. She hoped he wasn't trouble. Sybella needed him, and the last thing the town wanted was a bad influence. But then, his eyes, they'd seemed sad, his whole demeanour sorrowful and melancholy. But of course, it would be, wouldn't it? She remembered his condition this morning and her guts churned, but instead of judging him she'd turn her mind to how she might help.

But now arriving home, she felt edgy and behind schedule. Always so much to do.

Bridie creaked open the front door, hoping beyond hope that she didn't need to be quiet. But before the door was ajar to reveal their humble living area, she heard the soft snoring.

Her heart sank like a leaden lump to her stomach, and she braced, breathing deeply to calm herself. Taking tiny steps, she entered the room and clicked the door shut. Her father sat hunched over in the armchair he'd slept in last night. She guessed if she was a better daughter, she'd have hauled him into bed and made him comfortable. But really? The man weighed a tonne and for sure her back would ache for days after. There were limits, after all.

Pausing in front of him, she took in his haggard features and sunken skin, the grey whiskers lining his chin. She moved closer, recoiling at the stench of him. Gently, she removed one boot, then the other. Yanking the crocheted rug from the couch, she placed it across his lap and legs. It was cool in this room where the winter sun didn't quite reach through the flimsy curtains.

In the kitchen she put the kettle on to boil and whipped up a batch of her father's favourite cookies. He'd wake later and be ravenous. She wondered if their new celebrity chef baked as well as he cooked. How did she know he was famous? Roberta hadn't said, someone else must have told her but she couldn't remember who. He was certainly an enigma. A tall dark, moody stranger arriving in their town; it was like a scene from a book and Bridie smiled. Her smile slipped as she remembered he'd hardly spoken at the tuck-shop as they worked side by side. She'd tried, maybe she talked too much, probably had; she usually did.

In between sips of tea, she placed the tray of biscuits into the oven before filling a glass of water and popping out more paracetamol and placing them on the coffee table to her father's left. She'd place the cookies next to them. A proper meal would have to wait until dinner.

En route back to the kitchen she passed her study. It was a mistake, but she entered and fingered the corners of the manuscript on her desk. Bridie was immersed in this story; she could feel its brilliance and knew it would be successful. You could always tell. She was so excited to be a part of its production. Could she do a little now? Her toes crunched up and she leaned forward, as if the manuscript had a force of its own, dragging her towards it. Oh, she wanted to, couldn't wait to get back into the lives of those characters, live in the world of the words, the French verbs and the joy of trans-lating paragraph after paragraph.

It was mid-week and time to perform her 'day' job. That had always been the agreement. She worked in the farm shop with its assortment of strawberry flavoured produce on the weekends and during the week was her time to work.

But with her father out of action again, the farm beckoned, she could hear it whispering to her. It was being neglected and it was up to her. Bridie glanced out the window. She loved that view, a clear path to the patches of bright red strawberries, row after row. The years had dwindled their patch. In some ways it was a mercy, they could hardly manage what they had. As always, duty called first. It was ironic though, because whilst the berry patch was her first priority, it was the French translation of manuscripts that kept them afloat. And kept her working almost twenty-four seven. No point whinging. With a heavy sigh, she left the room.

The timer on the oven binged and she savoured the aroma of home-baking. Like a real home, a real family.

* * *

BRUSQUE KNOCKING ROUSED CALEB. HE SHIFTED HIS HEAD AND groaned as shooting pain raced up his neck. That'd teach him for crashing on the couch. The knocking continued, and he rose out of his chair and laboured towards the door, bleary-eyed and groggy from his deep slumber.

'Well, hello there.'

The voice was too high-pitched, the woman's smile too bright with extra white teeth and flashing eyes.

He squinted at the assault to his senses.

'I'm Jacqueline Kennedy,' she laughed, 'yes, just like the first lady, I'm the first lady of Bellethorpe. The mayor, that is. Welcome to town,' and she handed over a tray of chocolate brownies, the plate still warm.

She bustled past him without an invitation and headed straight for the kitchen where Caleb heard the rattle of cups and the rush of the tap and the incessant talking. 'I can't thank you enough for helping out at school this morning. That's what it's like around here, we all pitch in. But all the better that you're actually a chef. Well, I fancy! Too good for the canteen of course, but the thing is, poor Polly is out for the week, sick, you see, with a stomach bug. We're always stretched to get the help we need, and given you've recently arrived, and I assume you haven't made many arrangements yet, can you help this week? Here's the roster.'

Caleb arrived in the kitchen and put down the brownies. In one hand she shoved a cup of instant coffee and in the other, the piece of paper.

'You won't be alone. There are other volunteers,' she said and took a sip of her own drink. 'And agreeing to cook for the festival, you've made quite the splash into town.'

The taste of the bland, watery instant burned as it slid down his throat. It tasted vile but the heat warmed his insides and he immediately felt better.

'I can see you need some time to sort yourself out, and as you can imagine I have a million things to do. But please sing out if you need anything and the school will see you tomorrow.' With that Jacqueline patted him on the shoulder and left.

Caleb's head spun. This town was something else. He slumped back into the sofa and held the warm cup in his hands. Awake now, he took a moment to examine the room. It was simply furnished but oozed warmth and comfort. It was nothing like his top floor apartment in Sydney with its clean lines and white walls. Here the coloured throws and cushions complimented the lounge which faced a traditional fireplace with stone columns on each side topped with a timber ledge.

Photo frames were displayed on a round silky oak table in the corner with a white vase filled with coloured flowers. The photos were of Sybella with a gummy grin and bright baby eyes. While being chic, the room was also worn and ordinary. But he could picture his sister here. Another shooting pain zoomed across his chest.

His phone buzzed from somewhere and he searched his pockets. The hum sounded nearby, and he moved the cushions of the couch and pushed his fingers in the crevices before retrieving it. His stomach churned as he checked the screen. Marco, his business partner, again. Another missed call and message. He swiped out and the news flashed up. He hated that bloody function. If he wanted the news, he'd read the paper or put on the television. Too late, top story and it was still all about him.

Another knock landed on the door. Jeez, these people didn't leave you alone, did they? But before he could react, the door swung open and Sybella raced in, dumping her school bag in the hall before rushing over to him.

3

Like a little whirlwind, the five-year-old wrapped herself around his torso. 'Uncle Caleb, you forgot to pick me up from school again!' she squealed, pulled back and punched him on the arm.

Shit! He was seriously failing at this parenting gig.

He hung his head, reeling from the embrace and fought the urge to have the waif-thin girl back in his arms. He hadn't had a soul-crunching feel-good hug in ages, and it felt amazing. It'd be weird right, to drag the kid back in for another one. Instead, he collapsed into a heap onto the couch from her light-weight box. Sybella giggled and pummelled him in the chest with closed fists. The force was like a massage against his skin, but he made the appropriate wounded noises.

Bridie wandered into the room and offered a diminutive wave, ceasing their antics.

'You here again?' he didn't mean to sound unkind.

''Fraid so. I was at school anyway. I can pick Sybella up anytime, it's no trouble.'

Was he supposed to thank her for interfering?

'Mummy never forgot to pick me up from school,' Sybella said, her lip wobbling.

'But it's across the road and around the corner, can't you walk home by yourself?' he asked.

'I'm five!' she shouted, 'and mummy would carry my bag and sometimes we'd buy ice-cream.' She stamped her foot.

He was readying his reply when Bridie jumped in. 'Well, let's get some afternoon tea now then. Lucky, because I stopped at the shop and I might just have some vanilla ice-cream. Oh, and strawberries, of course. How about we have ice-cream and berries?'

'Yum!' Sybella jumped up and down on the spot. Okay, lesson number one: you could bribe the kid with food.

'Sybella why don't you take this bag for me and head to the kitchen?' The girl dutifully obeyed.

With her gaze steady on him, Bridie walked over and collected the empty whiskey bottle stashed in the corner crevice of the couch and in a rather robotic manoeuvre with a straight back and dead-pan face, deposited it into her leather handbag without uttering a word.

Caleb swivelled his head left and right for further evidence of his day. There was only the one bottle; he sighed. Clatter came from the kitchen, and he wandered in. Bridie handed him a fizzy orange drink and his eyebrows rose in question. She pointed to the counter and the open packet of Berocca. He nodded and sipped. This woman had a knack for ordering him around. And for having everything at her fingertips.

Sybella served up bowls. 'Want some Uncle Caleb?'

'Absolutely, yes please.' Sybella beamed and he melted a little bit like the ice-cream.

They sat down at the simple timber table and ate. 'These berries are delicious, some of the best I've had.'

Sybella giggled. 'What?' he asked.

She pointed at Bridie. 'Bridie owns the strawberry farm and makes the berries.'

Caleb glanced at her across the table and watched her sit up taller in her chair. His eyes moved to the large berry on her breast. It made sense now. His gaze lingered on her chest (it was quite happy there) but he forced his gaze back to her face. 'These are good. So, you're a strawberry farmer?'

'My father owns the farm. I've left you plenty for later.' She nodded towards the counter where trays of berries were lined up.

'Plenty for breakfast,' he commented.

'I have eggs for breakfast,' Sybella said. Caleb should know that. Lesson number two. Instead of wallowing in his pathetic life he needed to focus on this kid who'd lost her mother. What a twat.

'Guess what ingredients I've brought for dinner?' Bridie addressed Sybella.

'Is it for pizza? Tacos? Fish and chips?' the girl asked but only received shakes of the head.

'Spaghetti bolognaise!'

'My favourite!' Sybella shrieked. 'Thank you, Bridie.'

The kid had impeccable manners.

'Why don't we get started and Uncle Caleb can rest.'

Caleb made to object, but Bridie has risen ending the conversation. Damn, he'd been resting all day. Well, after downing the bottle of whiskey, that is, it had sort of knocked him out. And that had been exactly the intention.

'Caleb, I have some chicken soup for you because it seems you've been under the weather.' She pottered in the kitchen with her back to him.

Sybella turned on him. 'Are you sick? Is that why you've been laying around so much and always tired and your eyes have been so red?'

Bridie turned and leaned back against the bench, smirking. The grin lit up her face, something he hadn't seen before. It made her eyes sparkle and her appear even more beautiful. So, she had a sense of humour, either that, or she was having a dig at him, too.

'Sybella, why don't you tuck Uncle Caleb up on the couch with the television remote. I'll get the chicken soup ready and we'll fix dinner.' It was a ridiculous scenario, but it seemed easier to go along with the idea.

Sybella raced into action and offered her hand to escort him. On the couch, she placed a blanket across his legs and positioned a cushion behind his back. With Bridie's help, she delivered a tray of steaming soup with toast and turned the TV on to a games show.

'Family Feud! That's one of my favourites. Tell me what happens,' his niece said and together she and Bridie whisked out of the room.

He stared at the TV. Family Feud had been one of his sister's favourite programs too. The kid was coping better than he was. He watched the contestants race to beat the buzzer of their opponent and he realised this was the first time he could remember being sober with nothing to do: no rushing to collect fresh produce, no meal prep, no dinner planning. At least drunk he forgot. He could forget that he'd lost his sister and his career in the same week. In only a few short days he'd made the most terrible mistake of his professional life *and* become a single dad.

* * *

SYBELLA WAS IN BED; TUCKED UP BY BRIDIE, OF COURSE. NOW she handed him a cup of tea. 'Didn't think you'd sleep if you had coffee.'

'You think of everything, don't you?' he replied.

'I try.' She paused before continuing, 'I am very sorry about Abagail. The whole community loved her, it's such a dreadful loss. You must be going through a hard time adjusting to everything. Please, if there is anyway I can help, let me know.'

He stared. Hadn't she already helped in every way possible?

'You know with caring for Sybella, making meals, house-work, whatever.'

'I'm a chef,' he joked.

She didn't laugh. 'Have you been able to get away from work? You run a restaurant, don't you?'

He looked across the room at the blazing fire. The room was warm and suddenly too small. Bridie had lit the fire too, she was exceptionally capable, he'd give her that.

When he didn't reply, she said, 'Have you decided what you're going to do? Are you staying here or taking Sybella to Sydney?'

He shook his head. Caleb was lucky to get through each day at present. When he chanced a glance back at her, he read pity in her eyes. This woman felt sorry for him. Had he become such a pathetic mess that he needed do-gooders helping him out? He'd always been self-sufficient and had prided himself on it. Things had simply got on top of him, that's all. And it would seem in this little backwater it was hard to hide.

She was a damn fine bleeding heart, he had to admit. He thought country chicks wore checked flannelette shirts with dirty jeans and those ghastly workman's boots. Bridie's boots were rather stylish, and she appeared more from the pages of a fashion magazine than off the land. But then, she did say her father was the farmer.

'Here's the information about the tuckshop: the hours, menu and volunteer roster for each day.' She proffered him a piece of A4 paper.

He took it but said, 'Can't you do it?'

She looked at him and her face danced in the shadows from the heat of the fire. Gone was the humour of before, the softness, now she was officious and serious again. 'Yes, of course I can. And I will if you don't. Most mums care for young children in addition to helping their husbands on their properties, so it's not fair to burden them with another job.'

'But it's fair to burden you?'

'I don't mind.' Her response was automatic, but he sensed a hesitancy. She checked her watch and gave out a small, almost indiscernible sigh. He wouldn't say he was a great judge of character, but he sensed Bridie had a fair bit riding on her shoulders.

In a rare move for him, he felt the need to reassure her. 'I'll do it, but only this week while the other woman is sick, and I won't cook.'

Her eyes roamed his face, searching for answers. When she didn't find them, she smiled, and for that it was almost worth it. But secretly his head churned with ideas of how to get out of this ridiculous charade of the school tuckshop.

* * *

CALEB HAD SPENT HIS ENTIRE LIFE IN A KITCHEN. THE EARLY days were over a sink of piping hot sudsy water, cleaning stacks of dirty dishes until the soft skin had peeled away from his fingers. Then he'd secured his apprenticeship and spent days cutting only tomatoes. Eventually, he moved on to the next station and cut a variety of vegetables. The first kitchens he'd worked in had been simple and drab with only the most basic of equipment, but later, he experienced elaborate set-ups with a plethora of the best appliances. One thing in common, no matter the kitchen- the noise, chaos and the abuse, was the same.

His body temperature rose with the heat of the cooktop. He couldn't remember the last time he'd been in a kitchen and hadn't been half-tanked. Drinking and cooking went together, there wasn't one without the other, well not for a long-time anyway. It was all innocent fun at first, a drink to get through the busy service. Then a glass of something stronger to deal with the pressure. But the pressure had kept building until he was drinking an entire bottle off the top shelf each night.

But he was here now. In the modest kitchen of his sister's house where the early morning light streamed in casting a yellow glow. This was a simple act of preparing food for Sybella. He didn't need the drink. Despite the reassurance, his hand trembled.

'You're awake,' Sybella said as she entered the kitchen. Caleb had his back to her, but he heard the hesitation in her voice. He couldn't blame the kid for being tentative.

He turned, brandishing the hot pan and flipping the pancake. He smiled at her as it flew into the air and landed squarely on her plate. She giggled. Grabbing the leftover ice-cream and strawberries he created a stack.

'I've never had ice-cream for breakfast before.'

'I know you usually have eggs but there isn't any. I'll get some groceries today and you can have them tomorrow.'

'This is better,' she said and dove in.

'Wait!' He extracted his phone and captured a shot of the dish.

'What are you doing?' Sybella asked as he examined the photo.

Caleb paused. What the hell was he doing? Old habits he guessed. 'In the restaurant we'd take images of our dishes and I'd share them to social media. It's good marketing,' he shrugged.

Sybella asked exactly what he was thinking. 'But you aren't in the restaurant now, what will you do with that one?'

'Dunno, it was silly,' and he put his phone away.

'This is so good,' she mumbled through a mouthful. 'Are you having any?'

'I don't eat breakfast.'

'What? Mummy says you must eat breakfast each day.'

'Your mummy was very smart and yes, you should eat breakfast.'

'Why don't you then?'

The kid was giving him the Spanish inquisition. 'I always worked late at the restaurant, and I'd eat after we'd closed. I'd sleep late the next day and only have coffee until I was back in the restaurant and then I'd prepare myself a meal before work.'

That seemed to satisfy her, and she focused on her food until she'd cleaned the plate.

'Holy moly, for a little squirt you sure can eat!' he exclaimed as she licked her lips.

'I'm glad you enjoyed it.' He patted her on the head and she looked at him weirdly. Yeah, okay, she wasn't a dog. Lesson number three. He wouldn't do that again. 'What happens now?'

'Well,' she said, 'I have to get dressed and brush my teeth and pack my bag for school.'

'Okay, you get to it, and I'll clean up here.'

He was wiping his hands from the washing up when Sybella appeared back in the kitchen, bag on her back, dressed and ready. Her school dress was crumpled but he'd deal with that issue tomorrow, he couldn't become super dad in one morning, could he?

Opening the door, they almost tripped over a bright red ceramic dish sitting on the 'welcome' mat.

'What's that?' Sybella asked.

'It's a casserole dish.' He reached down to collect it. Lifting off the lid, Caleb closed his eyes and inhaled. 'I'd say that's beef stroganoff.'

Sybella leaned in too, screwed up her nose before skipping ahead towards the gate. Hoisting the dish onto his hip, Caleb headed out too.

At school he headed straight for *Bight Right Inn*. 'Oh, thank goodness,' Kathleen exclaimed as she rushed over. 'We thought you weren't coming.' She bent over at her hips and caught her breath dramatically.

'What's that?' she asked after recovering.

His hesitation was only a flicker. 'Today's special, beef stroganoff.' Her eyes widened and she whispered, 'fancy.'

Caleb hated being in the school canteen, their food was embarrassing. Sure, it fitted into their made-up categories, but they could do better. Perhaps he was a Jamie Oliver in the making? He squashed that thought pretty quickly as he slathered extra avocado on the multi-grain bread roll. Who was he to care anyway?

Bridie rushed in and his breath hitched. 'I'm ready to help,' she said and faltered. Again, she was resplendent in pink. He didn't realise he liked the colour so much. But while the colour popped, her sunken eyes were streaked red and she looked haggard. 'It looks like you're all organised,' she muttered, her smile off-kilter and less beaming than yesterday. Her legs still looked damn fine in her blue skinny jeans, though.

'I'm impressed. This place usually looks like a bomb has hit it during prep. What's your secret?'

He shrugged. 'No secret. A good chef cleans his own mess.'

Bridie opened the fridge. 'Wow! These look amazing.' She held up a salad roll and one of the fruit cups. 'What's this?' she pointed to the row of dishes on the bench.

Caleb bit his tongue. Anyone else and he would have snarled. For Bridie, he softened his tone. 'Beef stroganoff served on a bed of rice in individual cups.'

Bridie placed her arms across her chest. 'What can I do?' Her voice was softer too, almost a whisper.

He stood in front of her, so close he smelled berries mixed in with a hint of vanilla. 'It's all done. Go home and help your dad, or,' he realised he didn't know what she did, 'go get a coffee.'

Bridie glanced at Kathleen. 'I could serve at first break?'

'Sarah and Mabel are both here, so we're good today.' Bridie nodded. Once more, out of character, he wanted to rescue her, and he wasn't a rescuer.

She spoke first. 'You look better today.' They shared an unspoken exchange before she reached for her bag.

'I'll see you at the Bastille Day committee meeting tonight.'

She'd left before the words registered. WTF?

4

Bridie brushed past the people milling in the entry to the community hall. What the heck? Had she got the night wrong? No, she might be tired but was super organised and never messed up the details. Except, tonight the hall buzzed with activity. In amongst the fifty or so people present was a group of wives from surrounding farms. They stood in a huddle holding flutes and sipping sparkling wine. Wine? They never drank at meetings. There was also a selection of nibbles on a long side table.

She must have the wrong night.

Bridie searched for familiar faces and spied a few members of the local council, including Jacqueline, of course. Then there was Yvette, the bakery owner, Geoff, the editor of the local paper and every woman resident of Bellethorpe.

Something was up.

Bridie saw local schoolteacher and her dearest friend, Maggie and dashed towards her. 'Hey, what's up? Why is half the town here?' Maggie was also the secretary for the committee.

Before she could answer a hush came over the assembled group.

Bridie watched Caleb enter the hall. Maggie focused on the stranger along with every woman in the room. Bridie even heard their collective intake of breath. She had to admit she held her breath, too.

Okay, now everything made sense.

Tonight, Caleb's hair was still wet from the shower and hung in tight curls around his scalp. He wore a tight, plain black t-shirt with matching jeans and a shiny silver belt buckle. The right sleeve of his tee slid up to reveal the entirety of his patterned arm. It would not have surprised her if he'd ripped a motorcycle helmet off his head and dragged on a cigarette, such was his look. Except he appeared bright-eyed and rested but a scattering of dark stubble still lined his chin.

The man had to be trouble. Did that explain the butterflies swirling in her tummy at the sight of him?

Unfortunately, every woman in the room seemed to be experiencing a similar Caleb Stirling effect. A flare of irrita-tion shot through her. She'd met him and spoken to him, helped him, and hadn't simply gazed upon him like a teen at a rock concert.

Word had clearly spread about the newcomer to town.

The more confident ladies of the group wasted no time gravitating to his side, pawing him with their talons, offering him drinks and food, while flashing their sickly smiles.

Bridie directed Maggie to collect extra chairs for the

crowd and called the meeting to order. She was the President, after all.

'I am so excited to see everyone demonstrating such enthusiasm for the annual Bastille Day Festival. Thank you so much for attending. Lots of hands make light work, someone famous once said.' She smiled too broadly and paused for effect, wanting to drag out the moment. But she couldn't do it. 'This year, I'm pleased to advise Caleb Stirling,' she pointed which was quite silly because everyone clearly knew who he was, 'has volunteered to help.' Every head turned in his direction. 'Caleb, do you have a menu plan for the day?' she asked.

'Menu plan? Uh, no. Not yet. I don't know much about the festival or the requirements. Why are you celebrating the French national day – are you people French?'

For such a damn good-looking man he could be difficult. Or perhaps broody was more appropriate, or maybe sullen. She couldn't work out if he was deliberately rude or simply obstinate. Bridie plastered a grin to her face. 'Maggie, can you read out what food was available last year including the menu for the evening sit-down-dinner?' As Maggie flicked through her notebook of minutes, Bridie continued. 'No, we aren't French, Caleb, although sometimes we'd like to be.' A few people tittered. 'To explain, after the first world war, this area welcomed and resettled returned servicemen. Settlements were established around this region and the soldiers were given the privilege of naming them. They chose some of the battle fields as a mark of respect for their fellow men who didn't survive. You might be familiar with Amiens, Passchendaele, Bapaume, Messines or perhaps Fleurbaix, or Pozieres.'

She rattled them off in her perfect French accent. 'The towns were connected by a railway line built in 1919. That created jobs as well as many other industries such as orchards, farming and even a mine at one time. The railway operated for over fifty years before closing around 1974.'

The room was dead silent. The locals knew this history, of course, but didn't often talk about it. Bridie continued, 'Many descendants reside in those towns today and as a testament to the past, to the soldiers and the way they forged new lives and for those of us prospering here now and proud of the region and its history, an annual festival is held. People feel an affinity and connection to France. And what better way to celebrate than with French food and culture. It's become a long-held tradition and one that we love. It adds a bit of flair and fun to our community.'

Caleb nodded in a solemn fashion. Bridie couldn't read whether that meant he thought they were all completely daft (and that wouldn't surprise her) or he accepted and respected the past and the way it's always been done.

'Last year Chef Armstrong had stalls with frog's legs and snails, stuffed mushrooms and French fries,' Maggie smiled but no one else joined in, 'and for the main meal he prepared caviar, a duck dish with some fancy name I can't pronounce, and fish with cheese for dessert. That's very French,' Maggie offered.

'And did everyone enjoy the frog's legs?' Caleb asked the group.

Bridie jumped in. 'I'm not sure it was about enjoyment; it was an authentic French experience.'

'France is a country with some of the most delicious

produce and dishes in the world. Their food can be both authentic and a sensory experience.'

A shiver raced up Bridie's spine. His delivery was deadpan and bordering on patronising, but his words were like honey. She looked around and everyone was captivated.

'Great. You know what you're doing. What are your ideas for this year then?'

'Food is about a moment, a sense of place and time. It should transport you, be sensual, an unforgettable experience. Orgasmic if you will.' All of the oxygen was sucked from the room. He spoke to her and only her, his gaze intense, direct and she was inexplicably drawn to his words, his passion, him. Without blinking he held her gaze; it was like he caressed her with those dark, intense eyes. If a freak tsunami suddenly hit Bellethorpe, Bridie didn't think she'd be able to pull herself away.

'I can help you with the menu,' wealthy, married, wine maker Sally said.

The moment was broken. An over-the-top gulf of disappointment hit her. Caleb had seen her, really seen her and she'd felt alive, her nerve endings tingling in a physical sensation that rolled over her body. She'd felt important, singled-out and she'd admit it, desired. No man had looked at her like that in a long time. It left a pit of longing in her belly for more. To be loved and cared for and...when it ended, she felt it more keenly than usual, that sense of loneliness she fought to keep at bay. She lived amongst a kind and loving community, was very involved, and everyone liked her, but no one looked at her like that.

Maggie called an end to the meeting and confirmed

arrangements for the next catch-up. Geoff reluctantly agreed to run a piece in *The Bellethorpe Times* and quizzed Maggie on the details. Bridie heard the conversations but did not join in.

Caleb had brushed off Sally and spoke with Yvette, one of the oldest members of their community and the long-term owner of the bakery. The bakehouse had been a fixture of the town forever and so had Yvette. Bridie became present once more as she watched their exchange. Of course, Yvette was eighty and little competition. *Competition?* She must be losing her marbles. But more likely it was the first spark of hope she'd felt in a long time. Or perhaps excitement. Problem was Caleb Stirling was a drop-dead gorgeous chef suddenly the father to a five-year-old and he lived in Sydney. Plus, he was a drunk, and if there was one thing she couldn't tolerate it was an alcoholic.

5

Caleb entered the cool confines of the tuckshop with a sense of relief. Arriving each morning meant he'd survived another day. The commitment he'd reluctantly given the school canteen had him waking up each day with somewhere to go and something to do. Dare he say it had saved him? Nah, it was too soon for that.

'Good morning, ladies!' he sang out as he entered, noting with pride the time; he was getting earlier each day. He wouldn't admit though, that he'd grown fond of the old, basic kitchen with its bare produce on the skimpy school budget. Plus, he enjoyed the low-pressure environment and easy food prep. No unhappy customers was an added bonus. He'd even adjusted to Kathleen's easy humour and ready smile.

Today the air was still and the mood quiet, none of the usual rushing and easy chatter. Kathleen stood with a woman he hadn't met before, their faces glued to a phone, squinting to catch whatever the image was on the small screen.

The phone lowered and the two of them did a double-take, their eyes shooting between him and the phone. Kathleen's mouth dropped open.

His gut spasmed.

With surprising agility, Kathleen was beside him in an instant and the phone thrust into his face, so close, the image blurred. 'Is this you?' she asked.

His body stiffened. Bracing himself, he stared at the image that had haunted him these last few weeks: him, intoxicated, looking ragged after late service. Not his best moment but the one that had gone viral.

Kathleen in her usual bulldog fashion didn't wait for a reply. 'Did you poison all those people?'

Caleb held in his large, deep sigh. 'I didn't poison anyone...'

'Food poisoning, same thing, right?' she gazed up at him with large round eyes. The other woman came and stood next to her.

'It was an accident, a mistake. A stuff-up. I didn't know the prawns were off. It was completely my fault...'

Kathleen was doing that dancing on her toes thing again. She made a habit of that when she was excited or anxious. Which was she? Excited at revealing the scandal? Everyone else seemed to enjoy it.

'But you fed those bad prawns to a famous girl band and they were hospitalised.' The corners of her lips turned up in the hint of a smile.

'Oh boy,' the other woman said eloquently.

'Yes, that's one way to describe it. But not only did they get sick from the food I served, they posted on social media about it and they have a lot of followers.'

The other woman put her hands on her hips. 'How do we know you're not going to poison us, too?'

'Oh, this is Ruby,' and Kathleen nodded in her direction before addressing the woman. 'He's not going to make us sick, Ruby.'

Dear old Kathleen was sticking up for him! She continued, 'He's not doing any real cooking, only making salad rolls and heating up stuff. He can hardly go wrong with that, right?'

Okay, not defending him.

'Right?' she turned to him for reassurance.

'I have been a chef for over twenty years, and this is the one and only time I've stuffed up and the whole world learned about it. My career is ruined, and no one will ever come back to my restaurant.' His words were calm but cut like steel. But he wouldn't, couldn't, talk about it.

'Let's get on with the prep. The children will be hungry at first break. Ruby can you please wash the lettuce and Kathleen, you cut the fruit and I'll attend to today's special, mac and cheese.'

His words hung in the air. That involved cooking. Would they object and throw him out of the kitchen? Kathleen placed her pale, pudgy hand on his arm, covering the beak of the falcon and said, 'The kids will love that.'

His mind was a jumbled mess as he stirred the cheesy pasta. A tremble commenced in his arm and was like a shock wave causing his hand to shake. Since being in the school kitchen, he'd controlled his cravings. It was not easy, and today, it was suddenly unbearable.

He gripped his hands together to ease the shake. Did he really think he could hide away in the country, and no one would know who he was or what he'd done?

* * *

CALEB DIDN'T KNOW WHERE TO GO OR WHAT TO DO. ON ROTE, he headed back to the house where on the step sat three casserole dishes. Pressure pounded in his ears as the fury spiralled through him. With one foot he kicked those dishes. They crashed into each other, and he struck again. One smashed against the brick step and shattered. Grey, lumpy mince spread across the red concrete, mixed in with white mashed potato. One last boot and peas flew through the air landing in the garden. Over-cooked pasta congealed in a pool on the grass. He fought down his own urge to vomit.

Caleb couldn't sit alone in that house filled with memories of his sister and reminders of the shit job he was doing raising his niece.

So, he walked.

His sister's house was located on the high side of town, in a quiet street not far from the main drag, over a traffic bridge and flowing stream. Parkland surrounded one side and people traversed bike tracks. A building in the centre of the greenery had a large white 'I' identifying the tourist Information Centre. Surrounding it were well-tended garden beds overflowing with flowers in an explosion of colour.

The wind barrelled into him as he walked across the

bridge, like ice against his cheeks. He pulled up his collar and dug his head into his chest and strode forward.

He glanced up as he passed the French Kiss bakery where Yvette wiped down the counter. After that, he passed a bank, a pharmacy, a clothing boutique with white plastic mannequins in its window. The traditional post office had an elaborate clock tower soaring above the low-set buildings. Then there was the *Koffee Shoppe* – he didn't have the energy to cringe at the name. He came to a roundabout and in the middle sat a large bronze bell hanging from a crossbeam.

Caleb reached the pub on the corner and craned his neck skywards at the two-story structure and read a timber sign advertising *The Belle*. Without hesitating, he entered through the double-barrel doors. Inside was quiet for the middle of the day but a roaring fire enveloped him with its warmth. The publican nodded and served him with no fuss. He was on his third pint before the door swung open once more.

Caleb didn't look up; he didn't care who it was, the voices washed over him. A female talked to the barman about wine deliveries. He tuned out and sipped his beer.

'I knew I recognised you the other night.' A shadow fell across the bar. A figure stood too close, strong perfume circling. 'Not only because you're hard to miss, but your face was familiar. Last time I was in Sydney I had dinner at Lavapond. It was the best meal I've ever had.' He looked up then, eyes flashing.

Sally.

He remembered her name.

She placed her hand on his thigh under the rim of the bar.

'Lucky you didn't poison me,' she purred and caressed his leg. 'I'd love you to cook for me again sometime.'

A gush of cold air filled the room with the opening of the door again. The fire in the grate flickered. 'It is him, isn't it?' The voice was shrill. The new woman rushed over, and Sally removed her hand. This woman searched in her over-sized handbag and extracted her phone. 'Can I please have a self-ie?' She asked but the phone was already out and the camera function ready. 'Sally you be in it, too.'

The two women stood on either side of him and captured the image. 'I can't believe you're in our little town. Running away from the bright lights of the city, are you? I wouldn't worry about that little mishap, people will forget real soon.' The woman rattled on while photoshopping or whatever she was doing to the photograph, uploading it and sending it viral. Whatever. As fast as they'd arrived, they disappeared. Sally gave him a loaded look as she departed backwards.

Caleb downed the rest of his beer, nodded to the publican and left. He was grateful men weren't big on speaking. Luke simply saluted farewell. At least someone didn't care about him.

Next to *The Belle* was an old-fashioned sort of bottlo, meant to be a drive-through. He bought himself the most expensive, top-shelf vodka. Hey, if he was a celebrity, he may as well act like one. He gripped the neck of the bottle wrapped in brown paper.

* * *

'DID YOU ENJOY FRENCH CLASS?' BRIDIE ASKED SYBELLA.

'Oui, merci,' she replied with perfect intonation.

Bridie smiled. 'That's wonderful. Would you like to speak fluent French one day?'

The child smiled and nodded, and they exchanged a few more French words.

Caleb listened as he approached from behind. 'Hey, Bridie.' His voice sounded weird. Bridie turned to greet him, but Sybella rushed forwards and cuddled him tight around his legs before gazing up with her tiny brown eyes. His heart squeezed in his chest. He was all this kid had and she was so easy to please. Lesson number four. The kid smiled her toothy grin, and he wasn't sure if it was adoration or thanks. He gave thanks that he hadn't forgotten her today.

'Hi, Caleb. I wasn't sure if you'd be here, so I thought I'd take Sybella home for you. I also have dinner, save you having to cook.'

Caleb hid the paper bag behind his back and stared at the red casserole dish. There must have been a sale on the corning ware range at some stage. It had become his most loathed object. 'What is it?' he asked.

'Fish curry.'

Something different. Prepared by Bridie. For him.

A millisecond pause.

'Ah, brilliant… I love fish.' he said.

'Me, too,' squealed Sybella.

'Your timing is perfect,' he added. The sadness usually present in her eyes lifted and was replaced by a sparkle. He felt a lurch of excitement within.

'You'll have to eat with us, Bridie. It's only fair. Otherwise, you'll have to go home and prepare another meal and that's too much.'

Her facial features dropped a little then. Did she not want to eat with them?

'Well,' she said, taking in the two of them, 'that would be lovely.' She hovered, unsure.

'Are you hungry, Sybella?' he asked. She nodded and he continued, 'I skipped lunch and am starving. Let's head home now and we can eat afternoon tea after dinner.'

'That's very silly,' Sybella giggled.

'Yes, but I am very silly,' he replied. The kid just didn't know how much.

'Unless of course, you need to be somewhere else, Bridie. What are you doing here anyway? Shouldn't you be working in the orchard?'

'I run French classes a couple of times a week at the school, and I had a lesson this afternoon.' Bridie and Sybella broke into some French to prove the point.

'You speak French too? You didn't mention that the other night?'

'It's my father's property.' She paused and Caleb waited for more. 'But, yes, I'm a book translator.' The sparkle in her eyes grew brighter.

'Wow, that's impressive. In little old Bellethorpe you sit at home and write books in French. That's fantastic, I can hardly read English,' he joked.

Bridie transformed in front of him, soaking up his praise. Did no one ever compliment the woman?

'When do you possibly find the time? You're always here

at school or at a meeting or helping someone out?' Caleb shook his head.

'Yeah, it's a bit tricky. Someone always needs a hand.'

'Do they? Or are they used to you doing everything?'

Her reply was too quick, and he realised he'd hit a sore spot. 'I don't do everything, it's a community effort.' She walked away without further comment.

Caleb followed behind with Sybella holding his hand. A few mothers blocked their path and snapped shots of him with their phone. Caleb glanced at Bridie and heard her muttering, '*What on earth,*' as the women retreated.

'A newcomer to town is always interesting,' she said and kept walking.

She didn't know. Could she be the only person in town who didn't?

Bridie reached the house first. She stopped and glanced at the path and across the yard and scorched him with a look. 'Didn't feel like shepherd's pie tonight?'

'I prefer fish,' he was quick and responded with like lack of emotion. Without turning her gaze back upon him, she said, 'Someone worked hard on those meals specially for you. Let's clean it up before they see.'

'Eww, that's gross,' Sybella tip-toed through the debris avoiding stepping into the mess. She raced inside once past the worst of it.

'I'm sorry,' he reached for Bridie's arm, working hard to conceal the bag. A swelling of emotion boiled up inside of him. 'I forgot myself. I'll clean it up. You go in and keep Sybella company and heat up the dinner,' his voice cracked without his consent.

Bridie's face was a patchwork of concern and that angst, that care, that concern, was for him. It only took him 700 kilometres to find someone who cared. Caleb slouched his shoulders and his lips trembled, holding back the tears. But he couldn't and the dam broke. It was the first time he'd cried, and the relief was enormous. The tears started silent and fat and trickled down his cheeks but when her arms encircled him, it was like permission, and he lost his control. Her grip was firm and close providing reassurance everything would be okay. Bridie offered comfort, relief from the pain he'd held inside, and those tears turned into ugly heaving sobs that racked his chest. Gasping for air, he clutched her tighter, and hung on.

6

'You know I don't care about your reputation or what people say or even if you're a drunk, but as Mayor of this town I'm responsible for my citizens.'

Jacqueline Kennedy stood at the head of the couch with her hands on her hips and glared down at him, as usual, with absolute disregard for his privacy.

Bloody woman. Couldn't she leave him the hell alone? He stretched out his legs, but one foot bumped the empty vodka bottle and it hit the rug with a soft thud. He expected a reprimand and braced, ready.

He was on the couch, again. Hungover, again. Damnit, but that wasn't the swear word he wanted to curse. His temples throbbed in unison and his throat was as dry as a desert. He wasn't surviving today. And Jacqueline blabbered on.

Caleb glanced at his watch. Shit. The room was too bright,

Jacqueline's voice like a jackhammer. He was late for tuck-shop and Sybella late for school.

'You're helping at school, and we've lined you up for the festival. People are relying upon you. This,' and she swung her phone around and Caleb saw she was on his Instagram page, 'cannot adversely affect the local community. We aren't a haven for people to run away and hide from their problems.'

'I'm here because my sister is dead.' He sat up.

That made her pause. Lips tight set, she glanced at the phone. 'You've got quite a following and at the moment you're being trolled. People are cruel.'

He ran his hands through his hair.

When he didn't say anything further, she kicked his shoe, her tone softer and said, 'You're a mess. Tidy yourself up,' Jacqueline pulled away the crochet rug he'd used as a blanket and folded it into a neat square.

Then Bridie barrelled in, making the tiny room even smaller. She gave a tentative wave. 'Sorry to interrupt.'

'Did you know about this?' Jacqueline shoved the phone in her face.

Bridie frowned. 'His Instagram feed? Boy you have a lot of followers.'

'No, not that,' and Jacqueline snatched the phone away and swiped at the screen. 'This.'

Caleb hung his head in his hands as Bridie took the phone and read.

'Putting aside the personal toll,' Jacqueline said and arched one eyebrow, 'this could be a marketing and PR night-mare. What are we going to do about it?'

As if she hadn't just read the damning article about him and his restaurant, Bridie lifted her handbag higher on her shoulder and smoothed her hands down the front of her white jeans. 'Well, first things first. Sybella is due at school. I have her clean and ironed uniform,' she held it up. 'And Caleb is due at the tuckshop. Caleb, you have a shower and I'll put the kettle on. Jacqueline can help.'

Entering the kitchen moments later, the two women sat at the table with Sybella who was eating a bowl of cereal. 'She likes eggs for breakfast,' he said and kissed the top of her head. The child offered him a sly smile.

'We could do a social media response or a series of posts about Caleb's life here in Bellethorpe, sort of like a counter-attack?' Bridie was saying.

'Yeah, that's a good idea, but our older residents aren't on Facebook or TikTok or whatever and won't see it. We need something that covers all angles, something to inform the locals that everything is under control,' Jacqueline replied.

'I'm not responding to that vitriol. That feeds into these people. The moment I post anything, there'll be a thousand negative comments.' His voice rose and Sybella sat up straighter. He softened his stiff stance as he paced the kitchen.

'Okay, okay,' Jacqueline held up her palm. 'It's more important to address it locally for the moment anyway.'

'I know,' Bridie started, 'we'll get Geoff to run a piece in *The Times*, an expose: Sydney chef arrives in town to care for orphaned niece, helps at the tuckshop and agrees to cook for the festival.'

'Hang on,' his hands gripped the top of the chair in front of him. 'Why do you want to help me?'

Simultaneously they replied, 'Because we care,' and 'Because the town cares.'

Jacqueline looked at Bridie and Bridie looked at Jacqueline and both turned to face Caleb. Sybella pushed her bowl away.

'And we don't want people to become sick,' Jacqueline added.

'You all finished? Bridie asked and Sybella nodded. 'Go and get dressed and brush your teeth and we'll get you to school.' The little girl rushed away.

'I'll talk to Geoff today,' Bridie said as she cleared the table. Jacqueline nodded.

'No more secrets,' Jacqueline said and patted Caleb's arm. 'Let us help you for goodness sake, that's what this town is good at.'

Jacqueline left and Caleb went over to Bridie who stood at the sink rinsing the cups. 'Bridie,' his voice hitched, and he moved to stand behind her, 'leave the dishes. I can do them.' Caleb remembered the feel of her arms around him last night while he cried like a baby, her kindness and hushed words of assurance. Embarrassment mixed in with desire.

He stood parallel to her back, so close, warmth radiated off her body and he heard her breaths. He reached for one hand and placed it by her side. His fingers circled around her wet pinkie finger, generating only the slightest of touches. Bridie did a sharp intake of breath, lowered her head. Blood coursed through his veins at the reaction to him and at their closeness. He imagined moving her luscious locks out of the way of her pale cream neck and trailing feathery light kisses down the skin until she shivered.

'Uncle Caleb, I'm ready,' came a sweet little girl voice. He stepped back, dropped Bridie's fingers, his heart hammering too fast.

Bridie wiped her hands and avoided his gaze. 'I'll be off too. Have a lovely day at school, honey. Au revoir,' and Sybella beamed. When Bridie finally glanced up, she nibbled her bottom lip and a flush of pink tinged her cheeks, matching her pink shirt. He fought to control his groan as she turned and departed.

'Uncle Caleb?'

'Hmm.'

'I know a way to get everyone to like you.'

'You do?'

Sybella nodded and gestured for him to come close, and he leaned over, and she whispered in his ear.

'You think?' he asked, and she nodded again. 'Can we make a plan this afternoon?'

'Yes,' she agreed, then said, 'I think you're a wonderful cook,' and she kissed him on the cheek.

* * *

'YES, GEOFF, I KNOW. YES, IT'S A BUSY TIME OF YEAR, OH, OKAY, the boating and trailer show. Does it have to be covered in this week's edition? No, I didn't realise. But this is great material for the paper. The whole town is talking about him and we can set the record straight.' Bridie scribbled notes while holding the phone between her ear and neck.

'Okay, when does your new cadet arrive? Soon, yep, that's great but not soon enough. It'd be beneficial to run this piece now.' She sipped her coffee, but movement caught her attention outside her study window. Her father was in the field. The phone slipped and landed with a clunk onto the desk. She grappled to pick it up and apologise but Geoff talked on unaware. Listening, she watched her father bend over and pick a bright red berry and pop it straight into his mouth. He paused, savoured the flavour. Her spirits soared as he moved along the line of plants and lifted individual leaves with loving care and attention. He picked as he went and placed the berries into the cane basket he carried and tugged on a few troublesome weeds along the way. At the end of the row, he retrieved the hose and pulled it off the reel and watered the runners closest to him.

Please let him keep going; pick today's berries and then at least, her only task would be packaging and delivery. She could manage that. Picking took the longest.

Not for the first time her mind turned to their previously thriving patch that was so large it required seasonal pickers. They could still do with the help now, but economic return on their dwindling orchard didn't warrant the expense.

Geoff said something and her mind tuned back into the conversation. 'Okay, no worries, Geoff. I understand we're all doing the best we can. Forget I asked, take care.'

Her father disappeared from her line of vision. She tapped her laptop awake and searched *Caleb Stirling chef Sydney* and her screen filled with results. The guy was a serious celebrity. Heaps of restaurant reviews, some glitzy party shots and loads of food images. Bridie stopped reading to gaze at him: him in his kitchen garb, in fancy suits with slicked back hair and surrounded by gorgeous people. Her body warmed.

She kept reading:

Major mistake and career ruined;

Doors shut on famous Lavapond;

Band girl, Powder Puffs hospitalised with food poisoning;

Chef under investigation.

Ouch. The media had savaged him and his restaurant after the incident. Fuelled by the Powder Puffs who were the unfortunate recipients of the bad prawns. Her stomach churned at the gross detail and photos the quintet posted. Too much info! And despite Caleb's massive following and staunch supporters, the girl band generated greater negative commentary.

Shit. No one liked to have a lovely evening at a renowned restaurant end badly with off food. Every chef's worst nightmare she imagined. As she trolled through the comments on both social media and in the news, her coffee roiled in her stomach.

But then, she was hit with a new wave of enthusiasm. She, Bridie Finch would turn this around. Starting with their own small community.

7

'You know there are rules about what food is served in the tuckshop?'

'Really?' Sybella responded.

'Uh, huh. You're supposed to eat, I can't quite remember, foods in the green category first and then purple foods sometimes and never the pink because they are evil,' Caleb said.

'Sounds weird. Pink food?'

'Well, the colours might be wrong, but the concept is right. Healthy foods are best and others in moderation.'

'Sounds 'bout right. I can work with that,' Sybella pulled a serious, concentrating face.

'I think this is the most marvellous idea you've ever had,' he told her.

'You don't know any of my other ideas!' Sybella giggled.

They sat together at the small, round table in the kitchen. Sybella drank a glass of milk and ate chocolate chip cookies. 'Can we sell these?' Caleb asked and bit into a biscuit.

'We should because they're so yummy,' Sybella agreed and chomped.

'Ah, but that's the problem. We need a menu filled with delicious but nutritious food.'

'What's nutritious mean?' she asked. Sometimes when Sybella spoke she had the slightest lisp.

Caleb explained.

Sybella said both teachers and students loved his new food at the tuckshop. Mrs Bingham only heated up frozen sausage rolls and pizza and made stale white-bread sandwiches. But now, it was fabulous she said.

Okay, he'd completely bombed in the five-star restaurant stakes but succeeded in the school canteen. At the moment, he'd take the praise.

Sybella said *everyone* would love him if he kept up his stellar performance (his words) because they already thought he was a complete dish (her teacher's words). And everyone would benefit because the kids were well-fed. And be one less job for someone else.

Lesson number five: the kid was smart. But he wasn't sure the convenor of the *Bite Right Inn* would agree with her summation.

'Okay, what should be on the menu?'

She shouted out some of her most-loved foods.

'Can you write a list?'

'I'm just learning my letters, Uncle Caleb, I'm only in prep you know.'

'Give it a go,' he encouraged.

It took a long time but eventually she produced a list, saying each item out loud as she wrote. He assisted with spelling.

'Okay. I love your ideas. But I'll need help because that's a lot of cooking. What should we make for tomorrow?'

Sybella's tongue poked out as she thought but then she shrugged.

'What's your favourite meal?'

'I love lasagne. It was mummy's favourite.'

'Did mummy make it for you?' he said and lifted a strand of hair out of her eyes.

'No!' she said and giggled. 'Mummy bought it and we heated it up in the microwave.'

'That sounds like your mummy.' He smiled but his heart was breaking inside. 'I miss her.' Did kids talk about their dead parents? He had no idea.

'Me too,' and her head bowed.

'Will you help me make mummy's favourite meal tonight?'

'Yes! Can you teach me how to make it?' she bounced up and down in her chair.

'Yes, and we'll make extra and that will be for school tomorrow.' Caleb took the sheet of paper and they worked out the menu for the remainder of the week.

'My friends are gonna love this,' she grinned.

They prepared their ingredients for the lasagne. Caleb pulled over a chair and placed it at the bench for Sybella. His stomach churned and the gas ignition was like a light, setting fire to his agitation. God damnit! The room spun and he held his fist tight, resisting pounding it on the counter. No, he wasn't anxious about cooking, was he? No, he needed a drink, that's all. Cooking and drinking went together but that was normal, right? He'd been drinking the night of the disaster, but that wasn't him, that was the prawns. A niggling voice badgered him - could Caleb Stirling cook without having a bottle of his favourite drop in him? Of course, he could. He wasn't in that kitchen now. There was no pressure here. Maybe he could have one glass? But he couldn't, not in front of the kid. Even he knew that wasn't right. He'd have to soldier on, cope with the sweat gathering on his brow and his shaking hands. It'd all be fine.

'I love cooking,' Sybella said as the large dishes slid into the oven. 'I want to be a good cook like you.'

He ruffled her hair, radiating a sense of entitlement. He knew he could do it. 'I should have been here to teach your mum how to cook. I remember she used to make a pretty mean chocolate brownie.'

'Yeah, yum, she did. But, Uncle Caleb,' her head turned down and her face sullen, 'it was from a box.'

'No!' He feigned shock and horror, lightness returning. 'I'll show you how to make brownies with gooey caramel and extra chunky choc bits,' he promised. Happy, she nodded.

'You know the worst part about cooking?' he asked. Sybella shook her head. 'Cleaning up! But it's always best to get straight onto it. A good chef never leaves a messy kitchen.'

'Okay,' she agreed.

'I also have to plan some food for the French festival. Can you help me?'

'Oh, yes! Is that the festival with rides and music and animals?'

'I'm not sure. That sounds like a fair. This is to celebrate the French National Day and I'm to prepare French food.'

Sybella took a moment to ponder that information, but the oven timer chimed, and they extracted the bubbling dishes from the oven.

'Uncle Caleb can I take some photos?'

'Of course, do you know how to use my phone?'

With his back turned, Caleb continued washing up.

With a cheeky grin filling her cheeks, Sybella flicked her fingers across the screen of the phone until she found his Instagram page.

* * *

'WHAT DO YOU THINK?' HER BREATH CAME OUT AS VAPOR.

Bridie stood at Caleb's front door and handed over the newspaper. The traipse through the frosty grass had left her feet numb. She tucked her arms inside her pink puffer jacket and wriggled her toes in her boots but never took her eyes off him. He read with his head bowed.

He took so long she stomped her feet as the chill set into her bones.

'Sorry, come in out of the cold,' he said and moved aside.

Caleb once again looked like he'd just rolled out of bed. Bridie swallowed. He wore a white stretch t-shirt with denim wash jeans and bare feet but still hadn't commented on the paper.

The thrill of turning up with the paper was disappearing fast. She'd stayed up late to finish that piece for the early edition instead of focusing on her own neglected manuscript.

Renowned chef leaves the bright lights of Sydney to care for his orphaned niece and pitch in to assist a local community.

It was front page; she and Geoff had argued about that. The boating and caravan show was a good sponsor for the local rag, but in the end she'd won.

It had taken hours to trawl the internet and gather the information she needed. It hadn't been a chore. She'd devoured every morsel about the life of Caleb Stirling; the bits that were open for public fodder anyway; then she'd agonized over each word, description, sentence.

'You wrote this?' Finally, he spoke!

'Yes.'

'It makes me sound so good.'

All her defences tumbled down. 'Caleb, that's because you are. Can't you see? Sybella adores you and the community is all aflutter about the hot chef in the school kitchen producing the best food they've had for years.'

'Do you think I'm hot?'

Heat rose up her neck and her cheeks burned; she wasn't cold anymore. Caleb grinned and she couldn't form a reply. He returned to the paper anyway.

'Do you think it'll work? People will trust me?' His voice always sounded like he'd had a rough night, either that or smoked a packet of cigarettes. Today it tremored with hope.

'People already do, but for those few who mightn't, their doubts will disappear. They'll see you for the man you are. For the man that made a mistake and paid a huge price. For the man that is trying to redeem himself and get on with life. Who has chosen to come to our small town and care for his niece, the only relative she has and not only that, pitched in and helped where needed. What's not to love?' Her voice caught on those last words.

Of course, she didn't express her greatest fear: that he was the same as her father. She hoped he wasn't.

Their gazes locked, his intense and searching, trying to read her eyes, test her sincerity. She licked her lips, her breath not quite reaching her lungs. His gaze was tender, soft and caressed her skin. The pit of her stomach tingled.

He couldn't be a drunk, could he?

'Uncle Caleb.' The shout came from within the house.

'Have a cuppa,' he said but his throat didn't quite work and he had to clear his voice first.

She shook her head. Bridie needed to get the hell out of there and get a grip. 'Heaps to do. Remember there's a committee meeting tonight. Have you done the menu?'

'Argh, no, another one? You sure do meet a lot. I'll skip this one…'

'No way,' she said with a smirk. 'It's getting to the pointy end, and we need details.'

He shook his head.

'I'll do you a deal. Come to the meeting and afterwards we'll go to the local French place in the next town. You can get ideas.'

Quick as a whip he replied, 'I don't need ideas.' Another pause before their eyes connected again. 'But to say thank you for helping me when you don't have to,' he held up the paper, 'I'll attend the meeting and have dinner with you.'

Her heart was galloping out of her chest. *Shit.* Had she

just asked Caleb out and he'd said yes? Nerves were already dancing in her tummy.

'See you tonight,' she said and broke their gaze.

* * *

'THE TOWN STILL CAN'T GET ENOUGH OF THIS GUY,' MAGGIE whispered, standing beside her in the hall.

'Déjà vu, huh,' Bridie said by way of intelligent reply. Her friend looked at her quizzically. 'Have you been bitten, too, hun?'

'Don't be ridiculous,' Bridie scoffed but Maggie laughed.

'Well, just saying that I wouldn't mind biting that cherry, too,' and like everyone else in the hall, she turned to watch Caleb saunter into the room. Perhaps if the guy walked normally and didn't own the room when he entered, he'd draw less attention? Perhaps if he wasn't so damn cow-boy good looking with his tight jeans and messy hair, then the town wouldn't be so interested in him? Bridie couldn't tear her eyes away either.

On the positive side it had the town's people turning up.

They reached the item on the agenda about catering for the festival. All eyes turned to Caleb, like a king upon his throne, his subjects waited for him to speak. And in true Caleb style, he didn't offer what they sought.

'The menu, Caleb. Everyone wants to hear what you've planned,' it was Jacqueline who eventually spoke. He remained silent, his features not giving anything away. 'And it needs to be approved.'

Caleb stood and stared them down from his full height.

Anger flashed in his eyes and his fists balled. It was the first time she'd witnessed his head chef persona where the critics said he was a hard arse in his own kitchen and there was only one boss, him.

She willed him to sit down and not wreck their hard work so far in repairing his image. Seconds passed and she detected him calming, his hands loosened and fell to his sides. 'No one said anything about approving the menu. If you want me to cook for your festival, I'm happy to. I'll stick to the brief and you'll have your French food. That's it.'

'I'll help him,' a voice sang out from the second row.

Evelyn. *Shit.*

Having relocated to Bellethorpe five years ago, she was still considered a newbie. Her Hollywood, old-style glamour still caused heads to turn. Tonight, she wore a vibrant green dress with her long blonde hair pulled back off her face. She matched him in the sauntering stakes as she cat-walked towards him. Bridie watched Caleb instead. His eyes narrowed as they raked from Evelyn's toes to her head.

'Oh, that would be fabulous, Evelyn, thank you,' Jacqueline replied. What, no!

'I work alone,' Caleb replied. Yes!

Evelyn stared up at him from her diminutive five-foot stance. Height did not intimidate her. Hands on hips, she said, 'Before relocating to Bellethorpe I worked at an exclusive hotel specialising in French food. I know a thing or two.'

'Wonderful,' Jacqueline commented. 'We'll set up a time for you two to chat,' she continued.

The door opened and Ruthie, Caleb's sixteen-year-old neighbour entered. 'Caleb?' her voice shook. 'Sybella is sick.'

'What?' Bridie stood.

'She's vomited a few times now. You need to come home.'

Caleb grabbed his jacket hanging off the chair and shrugged it on.

'I'm coming with you,' Bridie said. 'Jacqueline, you take over as chair and cover the last few items,' she blustered as she rushed out the door.

Caleb turned and said with a parting jab to the group assembled, 'I work alone.'

* * *

FAR OUT! WAS IT HIS LASAGNE? IT HAD TO BE. HE PAID SPECIAL attention to how he felt, but his tummy didn't rumble, he was okay. But he was also famous for his cast-iron will. It wasn't his stomach, though, it was the ache shooting through his chest that made him ill. He and Sybella had been the only ones to eat the dish. Conscious of Bridie following, Caleb walked fast ignoring the chill.

'Hey, sweetie,' he said as he reached her bedside. Her forehead was on fire and clammy. 'How are you feeling?'

'I'm okay, just feel a bit sick in the stomach.'

'I'm so sorry,' he said as she retched into a bowl again.

Bridie came in with a wet washer and held it to her forehead and placed a glass of water to her lips forcing her to drink. 'You know what's great? There are special ice blocks for kids when they are sick. I'll pop out to the chemist and get some.'

Sybella gave Bridie a thumbs up, but her eyes were shut before her hand landed back to the bed.

Caleb followed her out. 'I'm sorry about dinner. I would have liked to try that place.'

'That's okay, we'll go another time. You're needed here.'

He placed his hand on her arm, wanting, needing to say more but he didn't know how to express what he was feeling. 'Thanks,' was all he managed.

Shutting the door on Bridie, Caleb strode to the kitchen. He collected the dish of beef lasagne from the fridge and shoved it towards the bin. The solid mass didn't move, and he rammed it again. The dish jammed against the edge of the plastic tub and spilled over. With two hands Caleb thrust the whole thing in and pushed hard for good measure, cracking the bin and causing the dish to shatter to the ground and scattering the contents across the floor.

8

'How are you feeling?' Caleb smoothed the hair off Sybella's brow. It wasn't clammy today.

'Much better,' Sybella replied and sat up in bed. The colour had returned to her cheeks and her eyes were sparkling once more. 'But, but, tell me,' she said, 'what did everyone think of the lasagne? Did they love it?'

Caleb didn't blink. 'I don't know, no one said,' and he turned his eyes away, suddenly very interested in the contents of her bedroom.

'What!' she exclaimed, 'I'll ask them tomorrow. I bet it was the best they'd ever had.'

Caleb kept his gaze diverted. He wasn't so sure the kids loved the frozen version he'd purchased from the local co-op this morning en route to school, but hey, who knew? It was much better than the alternative and that was poisoning the entire school community with his efforts.

'That vomiting was gross. Uncle Caleb, can wild berries make you sick?'

'Why do you ask?'

'Yesterday yukky Joshua Thomas dared me to eat a bunch of berries we found growing at the edge of the playground. He called me a baby when I said I wouldn't. I'm no baby so I ate them.'

She had his attention now. 'Did anyone else eat them?'

Sybella sat up taller. 'No one else was brave enough.'

He gripped Sybella's spare pillow tight to his chest. Was it possible his cooking wasn't responsible? A flicker of hope flared...but surely a few berries wouldn't make her vomit all night? But he guessed, she was tiny, a little waif of a thing. Doubt crept in. She'd eaten the dish he'd prepared only hours later; but he'd cooked the beef extra-long. If he'd had a drink, would it have been different? Too much coincidence...

Sybella touched him on the arm when he took too long to reply. 'Well, they could, I guess. It depends. How about next time you don't take the risk and call him a baby back for being an idiot?'

She giggled. 'Yeah, okay. It's not worth that gross sick. Next time I'll be braver and say no.'

Caleb didn't know what to do with that information. Berries or lasagne? A freak accident or his cooking? It was easier to think the worst. And no one was sick at school yesterday, so disaster diverted.

'As you're feeling better, I'm thinking we visit Bridie at her farm. What do you say we make berries and Greek yoghurt tomorrow for tuckshop? We can cut up the strawberries and place them in a plastic cup and top it with yoghurt and granola? Sound good?'

'Yummy, yes, except we need to use a recyclable paper cup, okay?'

'Okay,' he agreed.

He'd rarely used his car since arriving in Bellethorpe. It had taken an eternity to drive from Sydney but since then, he'd only walked the small distances in town. Except the *Finch Berry Farm* wasn't walkable but only a short drive away.

Dark clouds bruised the sky and turned the world a grey pallor; a gust of wind buffeted the car door as he opened it. Caleb hadn't bothered with a warm jacket but checked Sybella was wearing one. It was blue with stars on it.

'There's lots of fruit in this town, isn't there?' he commented as they passed *Appletree Orchard* with a large red golden delicious sitting atop a high pole. Then they passed a few wineries, that was more his style. He could taste the crisp dry white liquid as they passed Carrington Estate Wines and then next, Cockatoo Ridge Winery.

Less than five minutes from the CBD of Bellethorpe, the rain bucketed down in large, fat drops and even in the car the temperature dipped to freezing. Whether it was the ominous weather or being out of the township, but it felt like they were miles from civilisation and that sensation on his first day of entering a horror movie returned. If it wasn't for the scattering of low-set fibro farmhouses and long stretches of fields with a variety of produce, he might be on a highway to hell. Times like this he wasn't sure he'd ever get used to the country.

The flash of a bright red sign became obvious through the weather. Green letters advertised Finch Berry Farm and sure enough, next to it was a grand red strawberry so life-like it even had the pips and a bushy green top.

Turning where the arrow indicated, they entered a long drive lined with tall, majestic eucalypt trees adjacent to fields of yellow grass. As they moved closer, paddocks filled with lines of berries surrounding a home set in the middle. 'She has a shop here, too,' he addressed Sybella as they pulled into a designated parking area.

'Yeah. It's only open on weekends, I think. Not sure. You can do a tour, too and once they had a train, you know for kids. You're too big.' She undid her buckle. 'We're gonna get soaked.'

Caleb wiped the frosted glass interior and searched outside for any form of shelter. 'Hey, what's that over there?' he pointed and Sybella raised in her seat to get a better look.

A blob of pink bounced up and down in frantic movements. 'That's Bridie. What the heck is she doing out there?' his voice became a whisper as a crack of thunder boomed across the sky. 'You wait here,' he commanded Sybella, and he raced out of the car.

The rain belted down in heavy sheets, blinding him. His shoes sank into the softening ground, and he was saturated through to the skin in seconds. Reaching her side, he shouted, 'Bridie, what are you doing?' With jerky and fast movements, Bridie kept searching for berries and shoving them into the basket at her feet. 'Bridie!' he said and touched her arm that flung back in fright, the berry she held, flying through the air.

'What are you doing? Stop,' he gripped her arm.

Bridie paused and looked straight through him, her gaze faraway. 'I have to save the berries. It's going to hail,' her voice cracked, and she started franticly picking again.

Caleb checked out the sky. The far horizon was a steely grey but everywhere else was a freakish Armageddon green as if hell was coming for them. He lowered his gaze to the rows of plants. There were masses of red berries. The two of them alone were not going to save this row, let alone this field. 'Where's your dad?' he yelled over the din.

Bridie didn't reply but kept working. Caleb didn't know what to do: it was madness to stand here in the pummelling ice-like rain and pick strawberries, but he couldn't leave her alone.

Sybella arrived with spare containers. 'Here use these,' she said. He looked at her with incredulity before she said further, 'I've picked plenty of strawberries before.' Curly strands of hair flattened against her face and Caleb's heart couldn't help but swell. He bent over and yanked every berry he could see but before his bucket was even half-full, hard shards of ice hit him.

'Sybella,' he pulled at her arm, 'run and get under cover,' the little girl hesitated until a golf-ball of ice hit her on the head and she gulped.

'Bridie, Bridie, you have to stop, you'll get hurt.' He trailed behind her while she moved along the line with incredible speed. She filled two buckets and stepped, toppling a third.

'No,' she sobbed and bent to her knees collecting fruit from the ground where they'd scattered. Their hands clashed as they rushed. Once full, he held it close to his chest and their eyes connected. He shook his head, and she did too. He grasped her arm and tried to drag her away, but she stood rock-solid. Putting the container down, he tried again. She was like a stubborn donkey, locking her legs and refusing to move. Caleb was stronger though and eventually she gave way and he propelled her along. Under the awning of the old shop, she begged him. 'Please save what we've picked.' He nodded and braced himself for the barrage of rain and hail as he ran the few hundred metres back to the field, shoved every loose berry he could see into his bucket and his pockets until they bulged. He ignored the ones that fell as he ran.

He paused under the shelter but saw an open shed. He gestured for Sybella to move indoors. Bridie was frozen to the spot, so he settled Sybella into a blanket and raced back outside. Bridie was on her knees and sobbing. He grasped her under the arms, but she fought back with surprising veracity.

'No! Leave me alone!' She buried her head in her hands. Caleb looked left and right. Where was her father? The farmer? Wasn't he worried about his crops?

'Where's your dad?'

Her eyes flew open, and anger flashed through them, turning them a violent dark green, like the sky. He'd never seen that look before. It was hostile. Through gritted teeth she said, 'He's inside sleeping off his hangover.' Caleb took a moment to process the words.

'Should I go and get him?'

He watched her rage seep away; her shoulders slump and the fight leave her body. 'He's like you, a drunk.' There was no mistaking the words, they were loud and clear and said without the vitriol of moments before. Caleb took one step back, shock reverberating through him.

'He deals with life's problems through the bottle too. Then can't get up the next day.' Caleb reeled from the word drunk, but Bridie continued. 'Yesterday was a better day. He was awake and picked fruit in the orchard. I saw him,' a sob broke through her words. 'I was so relieved because it meant I didn't have to do any picking. But I'm stupid. I don't know what I was thinking. I should have checked but I didn't. He probably picked less than a bucket, perhaps ate the rest. Now, look,' her voice rose again, and she pointed towards the fields, 'if I'd checked I could have picked yesterday's crop and there'd be less damage today. The berries will not survive the hail. They'll be bruised, maybe good for smoothies is about all.' Her whole body shuddered.

Without thinking Caleb pulled her towards him, his arms encircling her frame easily, but she was a dead-weight. She shook and he held her tighter as her chest heaved, sobs escaping but eventually receding to small hiccups. Resting his chin on top of her head, he smelled the scent of her hair, it was all citrus and fruit and clean. Her plump breasts rested against his chest, the shape of her hips and limbs moulded to him; she was all woman and he fought against the bolt of pleasure that shot through him. His body reacted with lust; his heart cracked at her despair, but his head recalled her harsh words. Is that what she thought?

'Let's go into the shed, Sybella's there.' Bridie pulled away, wiped her eyes and nodded.

Inside he placed her onto a barrel with an old blanket

around her shoulders. Sybella offered a broad smile thinking the whole thing was a lark.

Drunk.

'Do you want me to go and pick some more?'

Bridie shook her head while tears rolled down her cheeks, visible now they didn't mix with raindrops. 'There's no point.' This woman who he'd only recently met, had been a constant ray of sunshine on his gloomiest of days, lent a hand to anyone who needed it and seemed to be the lifeblood of this community. Now she sat before him, completely desolate. Broken. He understood those feelings. But she'd been the one to help him, even when he thought he wasn't worth it.

Caleb Stirling wasn't used to helping others. He looked around him for inspiration. In the shed there were trays of picked strawberries and long benches with containers and water taps and other paraphernalia. He'd been in plenty of fruit and veg plantations and this looked like where they packaged up their produce.

'Sybella, do you want to help me prepare punnets of strawberries?'

Her eyebrows fused together. 'What do ya mean?'

'See these?' He held up some plastic tubs, 'we have to sort the berries into these for transporting to the shops.'

'Oh yeah,' she said, 'these are the ones we can take to the tuckshop.' He wasn't so sure about that anymore, he sensed Bridie needed these berries. Nonetheless, the little girl jumped up, ready.

Bridie shivered.

'I'll make Bridie a cup of tea first. Bridie?' he questioned.

Bridie watched them, her face pale and streaked with tears and dirt. Her damp clothes sticking to her.

'No, let me make the tea and then I'll help,' she strode over near him, 'thank you,' she said and stood so close their bodies touched. 'I'm sorry about what I said, I didn't mean it.'

Drunk.

He stared at her hard. He wasn't offended, shocked was all. Shocked she might be right. Shocked that he'd been so stupid and more appalled that she might be alone out on this farm managing everything while practically running the town. He turned his head to Sybella who was humming as she took close-up photographs of the berries before placing individual strawberries into the container.

It wasn't a discussion for now.

9

C aleb stood, stretched out his back and rubbed his aching muscles. It was early, too early and he wasn't a morning person. But the day dawning around him with its muted palette of colour was spectacular, except it was freezing. The sun hadn't yet reached the tips of the trees, nor did it provide any warmth. Caleb blew on his fingers to warm them up. Manual labour was not his strength, he cooked the food, didn't pick it.

Jacqueline worked beside him, along with a small but worthy crew prepared for the back-breaking work. He'd rung the mayor knowing she'd have both the people power and the persuasion to gather an assembled group to help.

'You've done a good thing here,' she said and rubbed her own arms to get the blood flowing.

'How did everyone not know that Bridie manages this place alone?'

For once, Jacqueline was speechless and her response

slow. 'She's so capable, no one suspected.' He'd confided in her on the basis she didn't blab. Wasn't gossip rife in small towns? He hadn't known Bridie long, but it was easy to work out she didn't want her dirty laundry aired, otherwise people would know of her plight. So, on the basis her dad was laid up, and because of the freak storm yesterday, help was needed to pick the decimated strawberries. And like he knew she would, Jacqueline had shone, and the arrangements were made before the moon was out in the night sky.

'Are we throwing these?' Jacqueline asked and pointed to the buckets of bruised berries.

'No. Give them to me, I have an idea.' The mayor studied him but simply nodded.

Caleb glanced once more towards the house. He hadn't advised Bridie they were coming, hadn't spoken to her after yesterday. Given she hadn't run through the field and demanded to know what was going on, and refusing their help, he guessed she wasn't in a good place today. He hoped she was fast asleep.

* * *

AT HOME HOURS LATER, HE SAT IN THE KITCHEN WITH SYBELLA, his laptop in front of them. 'You know 'bout the web, right?'

'Yeah, duh,' she replied.

'Right. Okay, search French strawberry treats or something like that.' Sybella stuck out her tongue in her signature move and typed with one finger.

'Wow,' she said, 'yum, yum. There's heaps of options.' He scuttled closer beside her.

'Remember the festival?' Sybella nodded and he continued. 'Okay, what we're gonna do is make strawberry desserts with berries from Bridie's farm and sell them at the festival. She gets the proceeds and the credit. Like those pink macarons, everyone will love them, right?'

Sybella nodded enthusiastically but said with a straight face, 'I think we need to practise and make these right now,' and she pointed to the screen. Caleb shot his look between the computer and her and after a few agonising seconds, smiled and agreed.

'And make extra for tuckshop,' she said as they were halfway through making the strawberry mousse, 'because this is tasty and it's made from fruit, so it's healthy.'

Caleb put his finger in the bowl and licked it. 'Absolutely, this is damn good.'

Sybella hugged him around the waist, her eyes wide and round. 'Bridie is going to love them!'

* * *

CALEB TUCKED HIS CHIN INTO HIS CHEST AND WALKED DOWN High Street. How did the locals manage these weather conditions? It wasn't just cold, Sydney was cold in winter, this was arctic. Wasn't Queensland the sunshine state? The lake he passed wasn't solid yet but displaying a thin sheet of ice and any visible blade of grass was unyielding with frost.

End of July now and he'd been in town three weeks.

Tucking his head almost out of sight was useful, though. He could hide from people (and thereby ignore them) particularly with his cap on his head, and his bare neck wasn't exposed to the weather. Perhaps he needed to invest in a scarf? But buying winter clothes would acknowledge he was hanging around. Was he?

John the greengrocer was setting up his footpath stalls as Caleb passed. Large and healthy oranges and carrots the centre of his display. 'Well done, mate, can't thank you enough. I've got a littl'un at the school and he's coming home everyday raving about tuckshop. You've sure made a difference. First, challenge healthy food for these kids, and then next conquer their addiction to computer games. You can't help with that, can you?' he joked but didn't wait for an answer.

Outside the next shop, *Pretty Petals Flowers & Gifts*, the owner, a woman he hadn't met before, rushed out from behind the counter wearing a bright purple apron and holding a bunch of yellow flowers. He had no idea what they were, but the scent was distinct jasmine, like he'd use in cooking. The fragrance conjured up memories and he batted them away, desperate to stay in the here and now. 'Oh, Caleb. I saw the article. Well done to you, thanks so much for helping our community. We can't thank you enough. And the festival, too. We need more newcomers like you,' she said before galloping like a gazelle back inside the shop, taking the delicious smell with her.

Shortly along the road he came to the *Koffee Shoppe*. These country people were showing him such gratitude, he'd forgive the cliché and kitsch name and see if they delivered on their promise of 'the best coffee in town.' He pushed open the door and a bell trilled. The place was buzzing, that was a great sign. But it was also tourist season with city-slickers in town for the roasting fires and winery tours. In the queue, women with prams smiled in his direction, and the kids running around high-fived him. A couple of old-timers sitting at the table in the front window came over and slapped him on the back. No words, just a nod of the head.

It had to be the article. Was Bridie right? Had the locals accepted him? His gut twisted. He didn't want to help in the tuckshop or be on the festival committee; he'd been bullied into both positions and never talked his way out of them. The persuasiveness of the town and its people had done him over. He'd only ever acquiesced with the view to getting out of both as quickly as possible. But he hadn't acted on it, that spoke volumes, right? And if he pulled out now, who would feed the kids and make sure the festival wasn't a flop?

Plus, Sybella had been so proud of him. That smart little beggar had known how to earn the hearts of the community. At the top of the queue, the barista smiled extra brightly, and he placed his order with his chest thrust out and shoulders back, standing tall. He ignored that it was a bean he wasn't familiar with. It might be local produce and the best he'd ever had.

His phone buzzed in his pocket, and he extracted it. His business partner, Marco, again. Feeling better than he had in weeks, he reckoned he could manage a chat.

Marco was momentarily speechless. Said he'd been ready to leave another lengthy voicemail message that would be ignored. Caleb winced. If he owed anyone something it was Marco, who'd believed in him and his restaurant vision and had invested his hard-earned money. His friend deserved better.

'What? How do you know where I am?' Caleb spluttered. At Marco's next words, the colour drained from his face like a visceral sensation. 'No, no...' he muttered. Forgetting his coffee, he rushed outside and scanned the street for a newsagent. Spotting it across the road, he bolted, holding up his hand and apologising to the cars he jay-walked in front of. Inside the tiny shop he held the phone to one ear and searched the pile of papers, disregarding the local rag and reaching for the national bulletin. It was at the back, a thick pile sitting by itself. Perhaps no one read *The Australian* in Bellethorpe? Marco nattered in his ear, but Caleb focused on the front page. A photo of his beloved Lavapond with its door bolted shut. It looked desolate and empty. He could handle that of course, but below in the corner, was a photo of him taken years back, looking young and fresh wearing his stripy kitchen gear and chef hat. Rifling through his pockets he searched for change and handed over a bunch of coins to the young girl at the counter. Outside the barista handed him his take-away coffee. She'd chased him across the street to deliver his coffee? Befuddled, he managed a thanks and strode back towards the park. He plonked himself on the closest park bench and placed the paper beside him, took his first sip of coffee. Yep, as he suspected, it was rubbish.

'Mate, it's not as simple as hiding away. I confess it's been convenient but I'm here for Sybella. She needs me, I'm her guardian now and my top priority.' He sipped the drink again as Marco replied and grimaced as the burnt flavour slipped down his throat.

'It's not quite that straightforward. I don't know whether I can uproot her and return to Sydney. You think I need to reopen? Seriously? No one will turn up...' They argued back and forth, and he kept drinking, at least the flavour kept his mind off the unpleasant conversation. 'Listen, okay, I promise not to ignore you anymore, but I need some time to mull things over.'

One thing he couldn't share with his oldest friend, didn't know how to express, was his feelings about being back in a kitchen. Despite the freezing conditions, sweat droplets formed on his brow, his arms became moist and the coffee roiled in his stomach. It was one thing to cook at home...

Caleb picked up the paper. It was savage and in stark contrast to the words written about him by Bridie. If she'd been kind, this male journalist was out for his jugular.

Fled with his tail between his legs from embarrassment and not heard from again

Resurfaces in dingy old Qld town, hiding perhaps?

What was once our most successful chef is now our most hated

How can anyone ever trust his cooking again?

And that wasn't the worst of it.... Caleb screwed the paper up into a ball before hurtling it and his paper cup across the green space.

* * *

BRIDIE SAW CALEB AND WANTED TO SCREAM, STOMP HER FEET, pummel her fists against his chest; wanted to release her frustration and anger. At him, at her father, at people who drank too much, hell, people who drank at all.

But she didn't do any of those things.

She watched him in the kitchen. He stood in front of the

free-standing cooktop and oven, muttering to himself before he seemed to lose his balance, lean to the left, connect with the wall with a heavy thud and right himself. Caleb took one step forward, paused and then stepped back, only to repeat the movement. Eventually he turned the knob and ignited the gas on one of the plates. He leaned down close and listened to it crackle awake. Bridie swore she saw his bare arms erupt in tiny, charged bumps. Still chatting to himself, he reached across to the bench where various tiny dishes were lined up. He threw into the pan what appeared to be onion and then a dash of olive oil.

There was no mistaking it, Caleb Stirling was drunk. And if there was any doubt, which there wasn't, the sweet sickly smell permeating the room was a dead giveaway. It was like a bottle of wine had been spilled over the lino floor and left to mutate. Not to mention the three or so bottles lined up in a row near the recycling bin. Not in it, mind you.

At least he liked to mix it up.

As he reached for another dish, he caught a glimpse of her, and he turned.

'Shit, Bridie, you can't scare people like that!' His words were steady; some people really could hold their alcohol.

'I'm sorry. I came to check if you're all right. I saw the paper.'

'Your plan didn't work, did it? The locals of this town might believe your glowing character reference of me, but the city folk aren't fooled so easily. They know the truth.'

'There's nothing about truth in that article. That's to mare your reputation and pick on you. They should be ashamed of themselves.'

Caleb broke out laughing, but it didn't have the resonance of a good old belly chuckle, it was hollow, and had an evil cadence to it. Bridie cringed.

'Yes, those naughty little journalists calling me names and ruining my career,' his arms gesticulated wildly, and his voice rose higher as his agitation increased. 'You know what, Bridie Finch, they didn't ruin my career, I did. One of the top chefs in Sydney and I served up bad prawns, rookie mistake. And I just happened to serve them to celebrities who now want my guts for garters. Everything they said is true.'

In response to his rising voice, she spoke softer, quieter. 'You're allowed to make a mistake. You're only human.'

'Making a mistake is letting your kid's birthday cake flop or the roast chicken burn on a Sunday afternoon. Not when you lose your entire business and all that you've worked for. That's not a mistake, that's a fucking disaster.' His body softened but too much because he had to grip the chair in front of him to stay up right. The pan sizzled behind him, and he turned his head slightly as if to acknowledge it but didn't move.

Bridie went over to the cooker and turned off the gas.

Roughly, he shoved her hand away. 'I don't need help in my kitchen. I don't need your help at all. No one does. You said it. You were right. I am a drunk, just like your father. I don't deserve your help, hell, I don't want your help and he picked up the ceramic dishes and smashed them one by one onto the ground.

Hearing the ruckus, Sybella entered the room, silent tears rolling down her face. Bridie drew the little girl into her side and held tight. Caleb collapsed to the ground amongst the shards of sharp glass and china.

Her instinct to help was overwhelming. She placed Sybella gently into a chair and moved towards him, placed her hand on his shoulder. He shrugged it off as if her touch repulsed him. 'Leave me alone!' he screamed, and Bridie jumped back in fright.

The curly hair that she adored, flopped across his forehead but he shot her a cold look, gone in an instant and replaced by regret. The edges of his eyes softened, the creases deepening and his lips downturned. He didn't mean it.

With every fibre of her being she wanted to stay, to comfort and reassure him. Make him chicken soup and clean up the mess and tuck him into bed and say everything will be all right. But a heaviness weighed down upon her, turning her body to lead. It was defeat and she felt it deep within her heart.

Caleb was an adult and intoxicated and responsible for the care of a little frightened girl.

Bridie whispered to Sybella and suggested she get her night things and they'd have a sleepover and when they came back in the morning, Uncle Caleb would be feeling much better.

But would he?

10

Caleb saw Sybella at the school gate and his feet broke into a run without his brain telling them to. The cold air cut through him like ice, and he struggled to breathe. He'd run over hot coals if he had to; nothing else mattered but her.

She wore a pressed school pinafore with two pigtails, her pink unicorn bag on her back. Seeing him, she bolted too, and they met halfway. He folded her into his body, and she snuggled in willingly.

When she unravelled herself, tears pooled in her eyes. 'You won't leave me too, will you? Like mummy?'

He knelt down to her level and held her in place with his large hands on her arms. 'I'm not going anywhere, you hear?'

She grinned and swiped roughly at her tears. He encircled his large hand around her small one and they walked towards her classroom, swinging their arms as they went. Bridie stood by the gate. As they ambled closer, she turned and marched away. Caleb's hand was mid-air in a wave, but she didn't see.

Relief swam through him and he gripped Sybella's hand tighter. His bloody temples throbbed though, so hard it thrummed in his chest. He was right worn out. He'd had many a bender before, long nights in the kitchen and drinking too much to deal with the pressure. He rarely drank outside of work, but that wasn't saying much, he was always working. Most times, a good sleep and he'd be up and at 'em doing it again the next day. But working wasn't emotional. The kitchen was his domain, he was king.

Last night was different. When he'd realised Sybella was gone, his heart had torn open, and he'd sobered, fast. Yes, his life had gone to shit but the kid had lost her mother, she was all he had. Caleb didn't know why he was so slow on the uptake. Stupid.

Forgiven, the orange orb sun in the sky brightened, his footsteps became lighter and his own problems were put in perspective. Everything had hinged on her. If she'd rejected him as a useless surrogate parent, he didn't know what he would have done. His new world, the one he was forming, would have crumbled.

At her classroom she asked him if he had stuck to their planned menu for lunch today.

'For sure,' he replied. In the early hours of the morning that was his only focus and he was now prepped and ready to serve up another tuckshop special. Sybella offered a thumbs up which was a lot more than he deserved. Caleb embraced her again and watched her place her bag on the rack and extract her drink bottle before greeting her classmates. He stood longer than necessary and soon she shooed him away, embarrassed.

Familiar with the narrow corridors of the school after almost a month in town, Caleb headed towards *Bite Right Inn*. He could even say the name now without flinching. Except unlike other mornings there was a flurry of activity as he approached. Extra bodies filled the kitchen and bowls, and utensils and food covered the benches.

'Ah, you must be Caleb.' A giant of a woman approached him, and his first unkind thought was of the Trunchbull from the Roald Dahl tale of Matilda he'd read as a child. Might have been the last book he'd read. But she didn't have either a mole on her cheek nor her hair pulled back into a bun. But she was rather severe looking and serious, one hand to her hip.

'I'm back. Thank you for filling in for me at such short notice, but I've got it from here.'

The words echoed in his head.

Over the woman's shoulder, Kathleen shot him a sympathetic look, but what did it mean? Was Kathleen sorry he was being ousted or feeling sorry for herself back under the reign of Mrs Bingham?

The convenor moved her hand to the bench blocking his entry to the kitchen. He wanted to continue helping but he wouldn't fight her for it.

'Right then. I'm glad you're feeling better, Polly.' Her left eye twitched at the mention of her first name. 'I'll be off then.'

Shit. All those pieces that had fitted back together so perfectly after seeing Sybella felt loose and shifting in his chest now. The throb in his temple worsened.

* * *

HER FATHER WASN'T IN THE ARMCHAIR WHEN BRIDIE RETURNED home. How ironic; she'd already imagined making him endless cups of tea, pumpkin scones and even taking off his boots and socks. One sole ray of sun streamed through a gap in the curtains and landed on the chair, colouring the old fabric in the most gorgeous orange glow.

For a brief moment, she imagined sinking into the soft cushions of the chair and letting the golden rays caress her skin. Ha! The stuff of fantasies. It took her less than thirty seconds to dismiss the idea as preposterous. What a self-indulgent thing to do in the middle of the morning. Instead, she put the kettle on and craned her neck around the window frame to catch a glimpse of her father. There weren't any berries to pick so what was he up to? The house was as quiet as a church and after a few moments, she heard the tinkle and crash of tools in the shed. Bridie reached for another cup and tea bag. Despite the stream of sun into the front room, the kitchen was cold. She'd make him a warm tea because the shed was usually freezing, too.

Bridie listened to the kettle bubble and slid her gaze around the kitchen searching for crumbs, dirty dishes, anything, to still her twitchy fingers. Is what Caleb said true? Did people not need her help? He might not want her help, but everyone else did, didn't they? Her father would be starving and wearing filthy clothes without her. Hell, he'd have choked on his own vomit by now. The primary school would be in a right pickle if she didn't take their weekly French classes. There was no budget for languages, nor culture; she provided that for free. And then the committees – the business chamber would not have a secretary, the creche wouldn't have a supply fill-in, the agricultural society wouldn't have any crafts for the charity foundations they supported, and God forbid, the French festival would not be a thing. And in times of illness, she weaned this town back to health with her chicken soups and hot drinks.

The kettle sang, its whistle piercing the air. Huh, she was most definitely needed in Bellethorpe, in fact, she wasn't sure how they'd survive without her.

Damn, Caleb. Bridie filled the cups and let them steep, gazed out the window. Why then did she feel so discombobulated this morning when she didn't have an urgent task to attend to? For sure, she could find one, but as if to prove to herself, she didn't. Her life was full, it was. But she was an essential service. Yes, that was right. Essential. What did Caleb think Sybella would have done last night without her?

She rescued the tea, shrugged her coat back on and headed outside. Her father was head-bent in the tractor. Today was a good day and she was grateful for that. He smiled enough for his cheeks to crease with lines and accepted the cup. 'Almost got her,' he said. Her smile faded, that old clunker hadn't worked for years. Was he losing his memory too?

On the short walk back to the house she reminded herself that today was a workday for her. Yes, she accepted that the French manuscript usually came second trump to urgent community tasks, but not today. Rinsing her used cup in the sink she noticed a chipped nail on her left pinkie finger. 'Damnit, when did that happen?' she cursed. But it didn't matter, did it? She had plenty of time and she resiled to redo both her fingers and toes before tackling the manuscript.

Her phone beeped and she flicked the screen with one finger to see the beginning of a message. Huh! She should shove that phone in Caleb's face and prove that she was indispensable. Rudy from the next farm had a fence down and needed her to keep an eye out for his missing sheep. Well, at least she didn't have any berries for them to munch on and ruin.

Bridie stayed focused on her task until her nails shone with pale pink polish. The colour buoyed her mood immediately. Clean, neat nails could do a lot for your disposition, she agreed.

Taking care not to smudge her handiwork, she sat at her desk ready for a full day of translating. Getting lost in the French conjunctions was exactly what she needed. Her mind was already returning to the last point in the story when her attention was drawn to a sticky note stuck to her computer lid. A reminder – *flyers* she had written in bright pink swirly writing. Oh yes, of course. She reached over to the four trays piled high at the edge of her desk and extracted the first sheaf of paper. It was a draft brochure advertising the French festival. Bridie collected a pen and poised to write suggestions for improvement. The nib was touching the paper, but she stopped. The brochure was beautiful – all the reds and whites and blues, a kaleidoscope of fireworks, and images of delicious French food. Well, that made her think of Caleb, damnit. Did it matter if the centre was slightly off or the words a tad too small? She was pretty darn sure if she put it to the committee, they'd adore it and approve it without a second thought. Why was she always so finicky? It was hard to admit but she did desire things being perfect, but they were her perfect. It appeared she had high standards. Perhaps good enough was okay. She replaced the lid on the pen and put the flyer to the side. Plus, it meant she could devote herself to the manuscript and be swept back into the beautiful Alps of the south-east coast of France.

But before she'd turned the first page, another message arrived, from Sue this time, needing a donation of cakes for a celebration this weekend. Bridie'd whip those up later but then she noticed social media notifications and flicked open the app. The farm had a feed and she used to manage it meticulously and post every day. Now it didn't seem worth it. No point driving tourists if you didn't have the produce to sell.

It opened at the last page she'd searched. Caleb. There were new posts to his feed. Food dishes of a lasagne and some sort of stew and strawberries. Oh, her farm. Against her wishes, her chest flooded with warmth at the sight of bunches of bright red berries. In the corner, only the slightest edge of a bruise was obvious. The shots were after the storm. She slumped back into the chair. There were comments and she couldn't avoid checking. Poor Caleb, he was trying to do the right thing and get his life back to some semblance of normal with the images, but the comments varied. Vicious trolls couldn't help themselves, but others were kinder. She touched the heart and clicked open the feed. *'Thanks so much for visiting Finch Berry Farm, come again soon'* and she used the strawberry emoji, three times. She flicked onto one of her favourite images of Caleb and gazed at it, a flood of emotions spiralling through her, none of which made sense. She remembered the feel of his arms around her, the care at which he held her, gentle yet firm, she had felt safe and cared for. What would his lips feel like against hers? Would they be soft, how would taste? He was right though; she cared for everyone else, but no one cared for her. Her father hardly remembered her existence. No, she was being ridiculous. The entire town cared for each other, and she was one of them.

The phone rang, shocking her back into the present. 'Oh, hi Maggie. Oh, poor thing. Of course, I can, I'll come straight away. Tell Rose not to worry I'll look after Nash until she finishes work. Of course. See you soon.'

With nails dry now, Bridie tidied the pages of the book into a neat pile. She'd tackle that tonight after dinner, maybe pull an all-nighter to finish. Then she could send it away and be ready her next assignment. She retrieved her medical kit with every conceivable item a sick child might require and rushed out the door.

CALEB HADN'T NOTICED THE TEMPERATURE IN THE KITCHEN DIP, but when he answered the door, snow flurries fell from the sky and melted upon hitting the earth. Shoving his hands under his armpits for warmth, he registered the couple in front of him.

He'd been deep in soapy suds scrubbing a pan when a knock landed to the front door. He'd startled, certain he'd heard wrong. No one in this town knocked, they only barged in with no regard for his privacy. But there was another rap.

Quickly, he checked the oven; the tarts and pies he'd spent the entire morning baking, were not yet ready. Baking was safe; baking wasn't cooking. Well, that's what he kept telling himself anyway. And given it wasn't cooking, he was sober, too. Did he crave a drink? Hell, yes, but he'd resisted. Another triumph, he'd proven to himself again it was possible.

'Mum. Dad?' It couldn't be.

'Something smells delicious,' his father said.

Perhaps he was drunk. There was no way his parents could be standing at his door in Bellethorpe, Queensland, Australia. Caleb hadn't seen them since he was fourteen years old, since the day they left.

It had been a day of reckoning. His parents announced they were moving to the Philippines to be missionaries; to save the world one person at a time. They'd always been God-fearing folk and attendance at church on Sundays had been compulsory during his childhood. Caleb hadn't minded, the supper afterwards was great. As a kid, he was easy to please. Until he wasn't. Until there were better things to do with his Sunday and as he grew, he no longer shared the philosophies of his strict and over-bearing parents. The division had been forming for some time before their declaration. Before they'd chosen to care for people that weren't their family. Before they'd abandoned their children and fled the country.

Abagail was only eighteen, slices of her leftover birthday cake still in the fridge. Maybe they thought having one child obtain adulthood was enough? He wasn't sure. What he did know though, is that they hadn't bothered with him over the years, and he had returned the favour.

Not like his sister though; she dedicated her young adult life to him; him who'd repaid her by not only by going off the rails, but out of control until he couldn't stand the hurt he caused any longer and he took off at sixteen and travelled the world. No high school leaving certificate, unskilled with a mouth to match. In those days it was a matter of doing whatever work he found.

But he would never regret those stacks of dishes out the back of shabby take-aways and restaurants because those places had formed his passion, his passion for food. And once he found it, he never looked back, only forwards. He'd climbed that hierarchy however he could.

There was no regretting his journey; it had made him strong, disciplined and once mature, he realised the pain he'd caused his sister. Upon his return to Australia, only those few short years ago after working in the best restaurants of London, he'd reconnected with her and seen her as often as possible. Now she was dead; but Sybella was here and she needed him.

Did his parents even know he was a chef? His father mentioned the smell…but yes, of course, his sister had kept in contact, as daughters did, he guessed, perhaps out of loyalty.

'Mum, Dad?' he repeated needing recognition it was actually them.

'May we come in?' his mother spoke.

'What are you doing here?'

'We've come for Sybella, of course.'

11

The earth titled beneath his feet. 'What the…' but he stopped. Not that it mattered, he could swear in front of his parents, couldn't he? He was an adult and an adult who swore. It was that niggling old thing called respect. He'd honour that niggle, but he wasn't convinced they deserved any respect.

'I'm Sybella's legal guardian. Those were Abagail's wishes.'

A ripple of laughter trickled out of his mother. His father's mouth spread into a thin-lipped smile but he didn't join in the chuckle. It was condescending and patronising and anger swirled in his gut. Without waiting for the invitation that wasn't coming, they moved past him and into the house and, placed their simple, small two suitcases in the living area.

'Where is she?'

In an exaggerated move, he checked his wrist, but he wasn't wearing a watch. 'She's at school.'

'Of course,' his father nodded.

'Let's have a cup of tea, then,' his mother said and walked into the kitchen.

Caleb remained silent as his father seated himself at the table and his mother put the kettle on to boil and wiped down his kitchen benches covered in flour. He watched them in a daze, as if the scene was playing out in front of him but he wasn't part of it. He sure wished he wasn't, this was a nightmare.

'Have you even met Sybella?' he asked. They both shook their heads. 'When was the last time you saw Abagail?'

'Oh, let's see. Before Sybella was born, I think about ten years ago.'

Ten years?

'And why are you here now after all this time?' Nothing made sense. These people who called themselves parents hadn't seen their children for years and now surfaced without warning and wanted to turn their lives upside down? His anger simmered below the surface, ready to explode, like mini darts from the pores of his skin, but he wouldn't give them the satisfaction of seeing him lose control. He ground his teeth together and curled his fingers in and out.

His mother delivered three cups of tea and sat at the table like they were having a civilised afternoon catch up. Somehow, he didn't think the tea would cut it. It was her who spoke first.

'Sybella is a child born of sin, a bastard, born without the support and love of married parents and not aware of God's love. She needs to learn the scriptures and lessons of the Bible to be welcome into God's arms and not repeat the sins of her mother.'

Caleb took a sip of tea that scolded his throat on the way down. It was exactly the jolt he needed to prevent the vitriol spewing from his mouth. He willed himself to stay calm, but it was bloody hard.

His mother wasn't finished. 'We're much more established now. Our accommodation is clean and comfortable. We have running water and our own bathroom. Unlike years ago, we were not equipped to keep a family in the Philippines. It was too remote but now we're in a proper town with a school and church, shops and other families.'

Ah, there it was. So, they did hold a semblance of guilt. It pleased him. No doubt, God forgave them for the sin of abandoning their children. He chanced a look at his father who sipped his tea unperturbed by his wife's harsh words.

'You've been baking,' he gestured to the oven. 'Abagail said you were a cook.'

That made him sound like someone out the back of the local chippie, or *gulp*, in the school tuckshop.

'Any chance we can have a slice with our cuppa?'

'No. They're for a festival in town next week.'

His father nodded, disappointed, searching the kitchen for another source of snack.

'Abagail was your daughter and a grown woman and a wonderful person and mother. At the age of eighteen you left her to raise a teenager when it was not her responsibility and she did a great job.' His mother went to interrupt, but he held up his palm. 'She did a fantastic job; it was me who stuffed up and made her life difficult. She moved to this town and made a life for herself and her daughter and was an important member of this community. She died of breast cancer, and you didn't return for her funeral or send flowers or make an appearance for your granddaughter then. It was the people of this town that supported her during her illness and cared for her daughter until I arrived. They are now supporting me. You've done nothing.'

His mother shifted in her seat, shuffled her feet. Caleb imagined the defences forming: it was God's will they had to help other people; they were chosen; the plight of others could not be ignored. He'd heard them all before and he wouldn't listen again today. Thankfully his father said nothing but looked to his mother for guidance. 'We have a right to know our granddaughter,' she said.

'Yes. But not to right any wrongs you say her mother committed or to convince an innocent child she entered the world in sin. That's, that's despicable.' He paused. 'Your job is to love her as grandparents dote upon a grandchild, nothing more, nothing less. If you can't do that, you need to leave.'

His skin rippled with tension and with the oven set to hot, the room was oppressive and starved of oxygen.

'We are entitled to see the child.'

'Yes, Father, you are.'

'We'll let her decide.'

'Decide what?' he asked his mother.

'Whom she'd like to live with.'

'She's five!' he exclaimed, and his father jumped.

The oven timer went off. Beep. Beep. Beep, breaking the tension. Caleb rose, removed the three dishes from the oven and placed them onto the bench. The aroma of baked straw-berry blanketed the kitchen, a sugary vanilla heaven. He heard his father inhale heavily.

With his back still to them and holding the benchtop for support, he said, 'I'll collect Sybella from school and bring her home. I'll tell her you're here and that you wish to meet her. I'll relocate to the pub temporarily and you can stay here and spend time together, get to know her.' He turned to face them. 'Do not brainwash her with your God-fearing ways. If you do, you'll no longer be welcome.'

* * *

'CALEB, WHY ARE YOU STAYING AT *THE BELLE*?'

Jacqueline entered the community hall for the last festival committee meeting. Twenty or so people gathered, much less than his previous presence had garnered. Had his charm worn off? Bridie ignored him, but at Jacqueline's words, she paused with her cup under the urn, mid-stream. Her head tilted towards them waiting for the answer.

Caleb set out the pink macarons on the white plate. It had dramatic effect and he liked it.

'Did you make these?' Jacqueline swiped one, ruining his artistic display of the French biscuits.

He swatted at her hand, and she laughed but still took a bite. 'Oh my, these are divine. Where's Yvette?' The mayor spun on her feet and locating Yvette sang out that she simply had to try them.

'They are for everyone, hold your horses. It's a taste test. If everyone approves,' he emphasised the word, 'I'll make them next week.'

'Okay, good distraction. But what's up?' she persisted.

Caleb shrugged. But that was for show, it didn't sum up the situation at all. 'My parents are in town.' He let that hang.

'Your parents?' Jacqueline sounded as incredulous as he felt.

'Uh, huh.' Bridie had poured her tea and stood next to them, listening.

'What do they want?'

Caleb told her.

'No,' Jacqueline tugged Bridie in closer almost sloshing her hot tea. 'They can't.'

Caleb wasn't sure what they knew of Abagail's history but gauging by the reaction, his sister must have shared.

He fingered the plate of macarons. 'They are staying at the house and getting to know Sybella. Hopefully, after a short period of time they'll return to their work in the Philippines. I can't image they'll want to be absent for long.'

Jacqueline grasped his upper arm and stared at him straight, their faces only inches apart. 'Caleb, we're here for you. Anything you need, please sing out. We don't want to lose you or Sybella, you're part of our community now.'

Caleb couldn't bear the intensity of her gaze, or her words and he turned away. He couldn't look at Bridie either.

Maggie called the meeting to order, and they sat in a tight circle tonight. Jacqueline insisted they start with the macarons which were devoured in silence. Bridie chewed hers slowly.

'Would you like me to make them for the festival? I think we should have a special macaron stall.'

There was a unanimous vote in favour. 'Can you make a variety of colours?' they asked.

'Yeah, I can,' he replied but he wouldn't let on at this stage he was only making one flavour - strawberry. He'd make up an excuse on the day for the lack of chocolate and coffee biscuits.

'I have drafted what I'd like to be the menu,' he held up a piece of paper. 'Shall we go through that now?'

Caleb addressed the gathered group, but his gaze landed on Bridie. As she watched him, he saw a contemplative flicker in the shadow of her eyes. They hadn't spoken in days. Was she feeling the absence as keenly as he was? He missed her, and dare he say, her help. What he'd always considered interference, he now realised was significant, but subtle events that made each and every day brighter. But, mostly, he'd missed her company. While she hadn't spoken to him tonight, he'd felt her scrutiny. Each time he looked up, she'd be peering in his direction, and quickly glance away with a flush of heat colouring her cheeks. Did she miss him too? He hadn't realised what a large part of his life she had become. Or perhaps when something is readily available you take it for granted?

He'd make amends tonight after the meeting.

Gosh, he was either surrounded by simple folk in this town or these people were the nicest he'd ever met. Each item he read out was greeted with oohs and aahs and compliments. It was one sure way to feed his ego—that badly needed feeding. Finally, Bridie spoke. 'I think that is the best menu suggestion the festival has ever had.' She smiled, warm and genuine and his entire body fizzled in the glow.

'The decision of the committee is unanimous. It sounds wonderful, Caleb, and we cannot thank you enough for contributing this year. You may become our annual French chef.'

The words were kind but cut through him. Would he be here next year? If his parents took Sybella he'd have to head back to the city and that thought made him sick. It had only been a few short weeks, but it didn't feel like his life was there anymore; and certainly, with his career in tatters there was nothing left for him.

'I know we are the festival committee,' said a fellow seated at the back. Caleb judged him immediately as a farmer with his faded and torn jeans, check shirt and hard-wearing boots covered in dust. But he didn't like to stereotype people. 'But,' the man continued, 'can we please pass a motion that Caleb be reinstated to the school canteen. The kids loved his food, they ate it, it was healthy and delicious, and no offence intended, but so much better than anything the wonderful Polly makes, even though I acknowledge she's been single-handedly holding the reigns for years with little assistance. My little Sam is now refusing to eat tuckshop since Caleb stopped cooking.'

There was a cluster of clapping from the group and Bridie wore a grin that spanned her entire beautiful face. Caleb held up his hands for silence and was glad when it took a few minutes for quiet to descend. The swelling in his chest prevented him from speaking immediately. He was chuffed but that wasn't where he belonged. 'I am very happy to set a menu and take people through its preparation. But the tuck-shop is not for me long-term.' The problem was, he didn't actually know what was, nonetheless he continued. 'I can advise Polly if she's open to it, if not, someone else with a passion for healthy food should take over. But I'm happy to be like a consultant, I guess.'

'I'll talk to Polly and raise the issue at the next P&C meeting,' Jacqueline agreed. 'Any other issues for resolution regarding the festival?' she asked. 'It's next Saturday!' she reminded everyone.

Bridie ran through the last of the arrangements – stages, entertainment, animals, rides. Caleb sat back and listened, glad not to be involved. Thankfully under Bridie's guidance, everything was well under control.

The door creaked open, and all heads turned in that direction. Caleb watched his mother enter. His heart accelerated and nerves gripped his middle like a vice. 'Heather?' he refused to address her as 'Mum'.

'Hello, everybody. I'm sorry to interrupt. Sybella is going to sleep and wants Caleb to say goodnight.'

He slumped back, relieved. Is this what parenting was? A gambit of emotions that sped through your body so fast you couldn't catch them. At the sight of his mother, he'd feared the worst. Now his insides turned to mush. Instinctively, he tilted his head and turned towards Bridie. Her smile was uncertain and small, but it was there, and it was for him. Sybella had to come first, and he'd go to her now, but he thought he and Bridie might just be all right.

12

'What are you doing, love?'

The chill of the early morning dawn held her in its embrace, and she shivered, right down to her core. Bridie tugged the pink beanie down to cover her ears and moved her hands in the fingerless gloves trying to retain some warmth. The sun didn't yet cover the fields in its golden glow and the frost hadn't yet melted on the blades of grass.

'Picking, Dad.' His grin infectious as she smiled back.

'It's Sunday, you should be in the shop. This is my job.'

Pausing a moment too long, he knelt down to her bent position at the height of the strawberry plants and placed his rough and thick-fingered hand on hers, stilling its movements.

'I'm so sorry for being useless. It's hard during July, I almost can't bear it. I lose myself because the pain is too great, the sadness overwhelms me and the only thing that helps is the drink. Forgive me, let me get through this time of year and I'll be right again.'

Bridie's throat constricted. She wished it was only the month. She seethed with mounting rage that her father had dropped the bundle and she'd been left to pick up the pieces, yet again. Bridie was adept at keeping her feelings locked tightly inside of her. How could she hurtle angry words at him, anyway? Who was she to understand grief and how it affected people? Her father felt the loss of their mother and brother from the tragic car accident years ago more keenly in July, the month of their death. Bridie's pain surfaced on a daily basis, but she didn't have the luxury of letting people down. And she didn't want her father to feel bad about his behaviour when anguish gripped him so heavily. Nonetheless words of forgiveness didn't slip off her tongue, nor reassurances.

'It's only early, let's work together for a while and then I'll head to the shop. You'll be due a cuppa by then, too.'

He removed his hand and the moment of tenderness between them disappeared. Her father skipped over a row and commenced picking. They worked in companionable silence until Bridie spoke. 'Dad,' she was nervous, new ideas had never been his thing. 'I saw on the internet that some strawberry farms are running 'pick-your-own' weekends and school holidays. They open up their patch for an entrance fee and people pick their own berries and take them home. You know, it's like a set fee per punnet. I was thinking we could do something like that. Everyone loves pretending they're farmers for a day and then,' she paused, 'given we don't have any help, that would help reduce some of the workload of picking.'

Her father had his head down and kept picking. It was quite methodical work once you got in the zone. You had to pay attention, though, because those delicious looking berries were deceptive, they required a tug before releasing from the bush.

'Now that's a novel idea. Would never have thought of it myself. If it works, we might be able to get the back field operational.'

The sun was an orange ball risen high in the sky now. Bridie wished it let out some love in the way of warmth, but she still shivered. She wasn't cold, though, not anymore, her father continued to pick and today he was open to her new idea. Mulling over her disbelief, she heard a car rumble down the drive. Could this day get any better? 'Better get back up to the shed,' she said and stood, stretching out her back. 'Come up for a cuppa when you're ready.'

'Don't worry about packaging these, love, I'll do that. You must have a story to finish, you attend to that during the quiet spells in the shop.'

Bridie almost danced across the field towards the house and shop. Let's hope their visitors bought out all their home-made jams and strawberry ice-creams.

'PLEASE UNCLE CALEB, CAN I HAVE THE DAY OFF SCHOOL AND help you?' Those tiny almond eyes bored into him, pleading. He'd told his folks they needed to clear out for the day.

Tomorrow was the festival and he had stacks to do and needed the kitchen.

His mother was quick. 'We'll take Sybella and go for a day trip, visit fellow parishioners in nearby towns.' Caleb caught Sybella roll her eyes.

They'd survived the week, so far. His parents were manically trying to convince their granddaughter what a life they could provide in an exotic foreign land, away from her friends, her school, the community and any close proximity to the memory of her mother. They needed to up their campaign, but Caleb wasn't going to help them. What had caused him such angst, now didn't matter. That kid was stubborn, perhaps she'd inherited that streak from him, because she wasn't having a bar of it. It made him enormously proud, but also relieved. Any battle he thought might have occurred over trying to convince her to stay, was unlikely now, unless his parents refused to accept her emphatic no.

Caleb prevaricated. Sybella had been a fabulous trooper, enduring many days with her grandparents. What would be one more? And he was going to be flat out. But he couldn't do it to the nipper, and he agreed to let her help. She squealed and jumped up and down on the spot while his parents looked forlorn.

He'd been baking for hours and had already produced 200 strawberry macarons. His father gazed at them longingly decorating the bench. Caleb pulled out his tart bases and let them warm to room temperature. He'd prepared the crepe ingredients and hoped the stall he'd arranged would be prepped and ready to go tomorrow without any hassle. The committee assured him there was plenty of willing helpers, too many in fact. Hopefully that meant Bridie wasn't doing everything.

The front door clicked shut and his shoulders relaxed. Sybella was beside him in an instant and he lowered himself to give her a big hug. Just the two of them again; it felt right. 'Okay, my assistant, you need to wash your hands and put on an apron. Then we're going to bake the strawberry cakes.' He fussed at the bench moving unnecessary ingredients and other items out of the way.

'How many?' she asked.

'I think we need at least ten.'

'Wow, that's a lot of cake.'

'Sure is,' his mind swirled with tasks. 'While they cool, we'll prep the ingredients for the baguettes, but they'll be prepared fresh in the morning. I have bakers delivering the French sticks before the sun will even be thinking about rising.'

'The food is going to be so good! Everyone is going to love you Uncle Caleb,' and she beamed up at him with one of those smiles that melted his insides and left him a gloopy mess.

'And you too, kiddo, my helper extraordinaire.'

They worked tirelessly. 'What are you doing with all those photos?' he asked her as she'd whipped out his phone once more capturing cooling cake slabs and tart bases while he sliced chicken and whipped cream.

She shrugged and he forgot about it.

'I'm tired Uncle Caleb,' she said mid-afternoon and collapsed into the kitchen chair.

'I need to sort out some serving platters and plates. Let's

pop these into the fridge to set and we'll find Bridie. She'll know where I can source some.' Sybella nodded, head supported by her hand. 'Tell you what, can you please taste test this one?' and he slid a fresh, small, strawberry tart across the table. Her eyes popped open as wide as saucers; her energy immediately invigorated.

Sybella rubbed her tummy as they left the house, still singing the praises of the tart. 'That was the best thing I've ever eaten.'

Caleb laughed. 'That's the finest praise I've ever received,' he said, wiping the crumbs away from the corners of her mouth, the only evidence of the treat she'd devoured.

The festival was in the local showground, only metres from their home. 'Sybella, is it always this cold here in winter? This town is freezing!' Caleb said as they walked. Whenever he'd left the house recently, it felt like the South Pole. The little girl giggled, 'Yeah, I guess. We get snow some-times and we can ski and skate!' The temperature must be below freezing so he believed the snow bit, but enough to ski? That he would have to see for himself.

To make matters worse, the sun slid behind a cloud and the world grew dim. He shuffled faster as a thunderclap rumbled the sky and forced the clouds overhead to rush past. A slight breeze picked up and the familiar fresh scent of rain permeated the air.

'Oh, no, not rain,' Sybella moaned but they'd reached the grounds. It was a hive of activity, people bustling to and fro, carrying tents and chairs and tables. Various marquees were set up forming a white tent wonderland. They wandered past signs indicating ticket sales, drinks, a bar and walked through tables and chairs scattered across an expanse of lawn. He spotted Bridie; she was hard to miss; a burst of pink in amongst the bleakness of the day. Her hair was pulled back into a ponytail with random curly strands framing her face, the bubble jacket was patterned with strawberries. She was a living, walking berry.

An unexpected wind gust swept the red check tablecloths into the air, and Bridie scrambled to chase after them. Rushing over, Caleb managed to save a couple. 'Do you have something to secure these with?' he asked. Bridie paused at the sound of his voice and turned, smiling but her body was ramrod straight. Caleb detected the strain around her eyes and mouth.

She stared at him for a moment too long. Was she happy to see him? 'Oh, thank you Caleb, Sybella, yes I do. Hang tight. I have a bunch of lantern lights for each table.' She disappeared for a second and then produced a box. Working together they placed the lights on each table.

'These look beautiful,' he said.

She gave him that contemplative look again as if she considered everything he said. 'The white marquees mixed in with the red and blue will look incredible,' he continued.

'Thank you,' she replied, her voice tentative. 'Would you like me to show you around so you're familiar for tomorrow?'

Before he could respond, someone yelled a question at Bridie, and she became distracted answering. When she'd finished, he said, 'Yeah, that would be great, thanks. I'm wondering if you have serving platters for the sweet food?'

'Oh, yes, of course. I've hired everything. You'll have

more than you need. C'mon, Sybella,' and she grasped the girl's hand and they traipsed across the grass. He fought against his need to walk with them, to clasp her other hand, hold it close, warm up her fingers, be near her.

They arrived at the kitchen specially made for a chef and industrial in its fit out and size. 'It's all yours,' Bridie said.

Caleb scanned the space, feeling a little bit like he was floating. His heart beat faster than it should, and his palms became clammy. All of a sudden, he was back in the kitchen at Lavapond. There was the noise of guests eating, drinking and talking, the clash of cutlery, the yelling of abuse and he felt the heat from the cooktop; it was all too real.

How can anyone ever trust his cooking again?

He flinched.

'So, what do you think?'

He heard the words, but they didn't register.

'Caleb?'

Sybella kicked him in the shin.

'Oh, ah, it looks as if it has everything I need. And clean, too.' Bridie stared, wanting more, but his lips were stuck together. Letting it go, she went to one of the open cupboards and extracted a handful of serving platters. 'This is where they're stored; take as many as you need. Probably best to bring the food over and we serve from here tomorrow?'

'How many people are expected for dinner again?' he asked as if she hadn't spoken.

Bridie paused, hand to chin in contemplation. 'Uh, let me see. I think we've booked for around one hundred.'

One hundred? The sting of bile rose in his throat. He swallowed and tasted the bitterness and sharp tang.

A man opened the flap of the tent and dashed inside. 'Oh, thank goodness I found you, Bridie. We're having a disagreement over whether the jukebox should be placed to the left or right of the stage. Can you please come and sort it out?' Bridie nodded and turned back to face them, pausing.

'You go, you're busy. We'll see you tomorrow,' he managed.

Bridie's lips parted as if she wanted to say something, but then she closed her mouth and left.

When she was almost out of sight, Sybella screeched, 'Bridie, the tarts are the best, you'll love them!'

'I'm sure I will,' she said and waved with a weak smile.

13

The crack of the lid on the soda bottle and the eruption of the fizz had him salivating. Back at *The Belle* that night, Caleb's hand shook as he held the glass and poured. The clear liquids mixed, and the ice popped. A squeeze of lemon and he took one sip, and the strong hit calmed him immediately. Then he downed the rest in one gulp.

The self-recrimination started immediately: *he'd just have the one drink to calm his nerves; to get on with preparation; to ensure he was in the right frame of mind.* Blah. Blah. Blah. It was bullshit and he was man enough to admit it. He poured the next shot before his brain caught up. It was gone in seconds too. It was like a drug - intense, immediate relief until he returned to a state of normal. Caleb needed to recalibrate his normal. But, damnit, he'd do that tomorrow.

In his dingy hotel room, rain drops splattered the tin roof and only served to remind him of where he was, and why.

Anger made the blood run faster through his veins. He was in town because his sister died, but the uncanny timing could not be denied. It was funny how his major life stuff-up thwarted the death of his sister. Bellethorpe was unequivocally linked to his career failure as he'd tripped over his own feet rushing into town to hide and recover.

And now, his parents had complicated matters. He wasn't at home with Sybella, instead, he was at the pub, again. Alone, with his demons.

Another drink and his mind turned in a different direction: the berating started. *What a baby! Just get on and do what you need to do.* The chance of poisoning more people with his cooking was practically near impossible. He guessed it was the 'practically' part that had him frazzled. He was a bloody good chef. One mistake did not negate the years of hard work and success.

How can anyone ever trust his cooking again?

So, yeah, he'd have these few drinks to calm his frenetic mind, and tomorrow he would make the best bloody French feast this town had ever seen.

* * *

BRIDIE LAY IN BED LISTENING TO THE RAIN PUMMEL THE EARTH, imagined the rain puddles deepening, the mud collecting and everything damp to the touch. Today of all days, on their annual Bastille Day Festival, the sky had to open up. If only she could control the weather too.

The drops on the roof eased and she rolled out of bed having hardly slept. She searched her dimly lit room for her wellies, at least they were pink. She'd need them today, even if the weather cleared, the ground would be soggy for hours. A craving for a warm cuppa was irrepressible and would clear her foggy mind. Cradling the mug, she headed outside. The sky was a grey blanket crowded with heavy, dirty clouds. She spied a triangle of light behind the hiding sun and hope sparked. It might clear. The best part of the day was towards the afternoon anyway when people relaxed with drinks and music. She breathed in and out, it would be okay.

Stall holders were setting up as she arrived at the show-grounds. Bridie released a sigh of relief at the sight of the marquees still standing and nothing damaged or blown away.

She was hanging the tablecloths out to dry when she heard her name and saw Sybella racing across the field. 'Bridie! I can't find Caleb. Can you help me?'

'Of course, let's check the pub.'

Sybella knocked on the door with her little knuckles barely raising a sound. Bridie pounded, waited, turned the knob. It was open. 'Caleb, knock, knock,' she made her voice light, but she was frightened of what they'd find. Sybella had no such inhibitions and raced into the room and onto the bed where a figure lay.

'Uncle Caleb,' she hollered and thumped his arms and back. 'Wake up! How could you sleep in today?'

Bridie stood back but heard a groan as the body rolled over. Sybella whacked his chest. 'Uncle Caleb,' she drew out the words and her voice cracked as if the five-year-old realised this might not be a funny joke.

'No. No. No,' she whispered but couldn't bear to look at

him. Her chest felt like someone stomped on it and she grappled to breathe and bent over trying to quell her rising fear.

She'd known. Who was she kidding? She wanted to believe, did suspend belief for a while, but more importantly, trusted him to do his job. That was why she outsourced. Bridie Finch wasn't a chef, thank God, otherwise she'd be responsible for the food as well as everything else. Deep down, she'd known she couldn't rely upon him. He was a quick smile and kind word but at crunch time he couldn't deliver. It didn't matter how many times she defended him; Caleb Stirling was a drunk. Maybe she needed to ply him with more alcohol, and he'd perform today, enough to get him through anyways.

Now she really was going crazy. Bridie stood up tall, her breathing coming easier. She pushed the disappointment away, but it was replaced by overwhelming, crushing defeat. Fatigue washed over her; from lack of sleep, from weeks of preparations, from keeping everything going, for being responsible. Her shoulders sagged with the heavy weight. Bridie wanted to curl up in that bed and hide from the world too.

But that's not what she did, was it?

At the lack of response from Caleb, Sybella cried. 'Bridie, he's not dead, is he?' That snapped her quick-smart out of her stupor. The poor kid.

'Sweetie,' she touched Sybella on the shoulders, 'he isn't dead, I promise,' and she guided the girl back to the edge of the bed. Meanwhile her gaze scanned the room for the culprits; they lay in a jumble off to the side. Gin was his choice this time and there were two empty bottles. That was why there was no smell. She'd learned a lot over the years from her over-indulging father.

Bridie zoned in to do what she did best, care for others, ensure they were okay and get on with things, by herself if she had to.

'Caleb,' she yelled and shook his shoulders. He roused, his face creased from a deep sleep and his hair tousled. She refused to listen to her erratic heartbeat, that was adrenalin, right? His bare arms lay outside the bed linen to reveal the top of his chest where a sprig of hair sat at the nape of his neck. A groan escaped as his eyes flicked open, she presumed the pathetic daylight creeping into the room made his temples throb. Good.

'Sybella, honey, can you run downstairs to Luke the barman and ask for a bottle of water and some aspirin, please?' She nodded and backstepped off the bed, her eyes peeled to Caleb.

After she'd left the room, Bridie leaned over, pulled the sheets up to cover his bare chest and unleashed her anger. 'How could you be so irresponsible? The festival is today, today Caleb!' Her intonation rose at each word.

His head lifted, and he rose onto his elbows with effort. Dazed, he glanced around the room, taking in the dingy setting and peered out the window. 'Shit, Bridie, I can't do it. I can't cook for all those people. What if I do it again?' and he fell back against the bed and covered his eyes with a pillow.

'You're a fool,' she said and ripped the pillow off his head. 'What do you think you've been doing? What do you call the food you've prepared for the tuckshop, for others, that you've fed Sybella every night? Is that not cooking?' she mocked him.

'That's different,' he pouted.

'No, it's not. You haven't killed anyone that I'm aware of. For God's sake, get over yourself,' and Caleb reached for the pillow again, but it was out of reach, and he pulled the sheet over his head instead. 'For once, Caleb Stirling, this isn't about you. This isn't about your career, or your fancy restaurant or how good a chef you are. This about community. A tight-knit group of kind people that celebrate together once a year. Do you think they care how you made the cakes? Or what you serve for dinner? They aren't five-star clientele but good-hard working folk. And you know what, they deserve better.'

Caleb remained silent.

'Argh!' Bridie collected the bottles and threw them in the trash with a loud clunk that emitted a further unpleasant sound from Caleb. Bridie stood with her hands on her head, feeling in that instant as if she might explode. Rage rolled through her once more. What on earth was she going to do?

Sybella returned and Bridie shoved those drugs into Caleb's palm rougher than necessary, but he didn't move. This was no time for nonsense. She lifted an unwilling Caleb to a sitting position. 'Drink this,' she said and forced the water to his lips. He took a tiny sip. 'No, all of it.' Her handbag left at the festival had her emergency kit, that'd sort him out, not that he deserved it. Today, she was pleased she couldn't offer him all the tonics in the world. If he was going to be so stupid, let him pay the price.

Once the bottle was empty, she lowered him down to the bed and tucked him in. Sybella watched on.

'Hey there,' she said and slid her hand across Sybella's silky hair. 'Uncle Caleb needs to sleep for a while, so we'll leave him be. Is all the food that you prepared at your house?'

The girl nodded. 'I helped yesterday; I know where it is. He told me about the French sandwiches too, so I know how to prepare them.'

Bridie flashed a tight, tentative smile. 'Ah, that's great. We'll be a team. First thing we'll transport the food and make the baguettes. Remember the long, narrow French bread is called a baguette,' her voice returned to its normal timbre.

At the house, Caleb's parents asked a million questions. Bridie was livid for sure, but she wouldn't make matters worse with his parents. She avoided the answer they most wanted – where was Caleb? Sidestepping beautifully, she placed a stack of boxes into Ian's arms. He spluttered and reverted to Heather for guidance, but she was similarly armed. 'Can you please help by carrying these across to the showgrounds? I can take it from there,' and she offered her warmest smile.

It took a few trips but everything they needed was where it should be. Bridie didn't want to admit but the sweets looked amazing. There was an assortment of tarts, cakes and macarons. Oh shit, she realised she'd forgotten to bring the punnets of strawberries. Man, she hoped her father was awake this morning. He'd promised to attend the fair, so she might be in luck.

Sybella placed the treats onto plates for display. Bridie did a double take. Every sweet was strawberry. 'Sybella,' she asked sidling up to the girl, 'are there any other cakes?'

The girl shook her head and her lips dropped. 'Don't you like these ones?'

'No, sweetie, I love them. I notice they're all strawberry...' her voice dropped, uncertain what that meant.

Sybella beamed. 'Yes,' she cried, 'yes, Uncle Caleb saved your bruised berries and made all of these, for you and your farm,' and she looked left and right searching for something. 'Oh, he wanted a sign too, but I can't see it.' She turned back to Bridie. 'You know a sign advertising *Finch Berry Farm*, so everyone knows where the berries come from.'

Hundreds of thoughts slammed into each other in her head, but none made coherent sense. For once, she was speechless.

Joel, running the drink stall, approached and sought help. 'Sybella, keep going and I'll be back in a tick.'

In record time Bridie put out spot fires: missing tables, location of equipment, introductions, checking playlists and pricing of produce. Racing back to Sybella, she noticed the clouds had cleared, the sun was dull, but present in a pale blue sky and it hadn't rained in hours. It wasn't freezing, either. There were millions of other tasks, but instead, she pulled up a chair once she reached Sybella and they made baguettes.

A miracle occurred over the next hour. Everyone left her alone, there were no questions to answer or decisions to make. People coped. On their own. One part of her experienced a pang of sadness, she liked being needed. She knew what the locals called her – the do-gooder, bleeding heart or good Samaritan. But she genuinely enjoyed helping people. It gave her purpose. But somewhere along the way, she'd become the only responsible person in town. Want something done? Give it to Bridie.

The other part of her was relieved that she'd enjoyed a break. What a treat! Bridie looked around the field. There were people rushing but they were happy and smiling and helping, having a great time. Reality check – if she wasn't here, the day would proceed with success. It was a team effort. *Ouch.*

Even though the celebrations were in full swing, she wasn't inclined to move. Sybella gave her a cold lemonade and she pecked at the leftovers from their sandwich prep. Man, that duck was good! Caleb the man who said he couldn't, could sure as hell make a great French roll.

'Oh, love, there you are. Where should I put these?' her father approached with boxes of their punnets.

'Dad, thank you,' and she wrapped him in an embrace. She'd forgotten to ring him, and he'd remembered. 'That's okay, love. I saw a spare gazebo over yonder, should I go and set up and see if we can flog a few?'

She laughed and it released the tension that had been bunching in her belly, hell, for years. Usually, she'd insist he relax and enjoy himself and she'd take over and simultaneously run three stalls at once. Something hard and sharp shifted within her. She could not do everything and why did she think she ever could? 'That would be fabulous. Thank you,' and she tossed him a money bag and off he trotted.

Sitting on a picnic blanket and listening to the band play, she helped herself to a flute of icy cold French champagne.

Bridie sipped the cool liquid; it felt momentous because she never drank. Would this lead to trouble? No because the rain had cleared and left them with a sparkling, bright clear winter's day. It was idyllic.

'Bridie, can you please come and help me?' Sybella held her hands in front and swung them side to side appearing unable to contain her excitement.

'Sure,' she said, and the little girl swept her along.

14

'You're a drunk! And not a fit carer of a five-year-old,' his father said.

'We read about what you did in the newspaper. Abagail said you were a fine cook, but a good chef doesn't make his customers sick,' his mother said. 'And look at you,' she spat, 'you're dishevelled like a common hobo. You stink of alcohol and look like you haven't slept in days...' she closed her eyes and prayed but he zoned out from the words.

Caleb held a pan in his hand and gripped it so tight his knuckles turned white. 'I don't care what you think of me. You aren't taking her!' He slammed that pan down onto the steel make-shift bench where it didn't make nearly as much clatter as he'd hoped. It hurt his head, though.

'Now, if you'll excuse me, I have dinner to prepare,' and he turned his back on them.

'Son, if we leave now, we won't be back and that child will

never be accepted by God,' his father said to his back. Caleb did not reply.

Light penetrated the tent as Sybella entered with Bridie. He glanced up to catch her expression. Astonishment. Caleb raked his hand through his hair. He didn't doubt his mother's sentiments, he must look like shit. But after the water had soaked up the alcohol and the drugs had kicked in, he'd got moving. There wasn't time for making himself respectable. He had a festival to save.

Seeing Bridie made him remember the gut-wrenching disappointment he'd caused. The look on her face when she'd seen him this morning would be forever etched in his mind; his guts churned as he recalled her reaction. That was all it took.

Bridie leaned down close to Sybella and whispered in her ear before the girl raced away. 'What can I get you?' she asked as she stood close to him.

'Are you making me a drink?'

Bridie spluttered, 'No! I'm offering my help or water or Panadol or anything else you might need.'

He cracked a grin. 'Well, I was thinking that one wee dram might warm me up enough to get through dinner.'

She twirled on the spot real fast, her face a mural of emotion. Her eyes searched his, darting left and right. 'I'm kidding!' he surrendered.

'Oh boy, I actually thought you were serious,' and she blew out a breath. It was sweet like the champagne she still carried.

'Do you feel all right?' she asked, hesitating, like she was scared of the answer.

'No. I'm smashed, but my head is now only a dull ache, so for that I'm grateful.'

'Can you do it?' she asked quieter again.

'It was you, Bridie Finch who told me I can. Are you having doubts?'

'Me, no.' She shook her head too forcefully. 'I think you're a brilliant cook.'

The words dried up in his mouth and he couldn't speak. He cleared his throat. 'I hope you have good public liability insurance,' he said deadpan.

'That's not funny.'

He turned to her then, stared into those crystal-clear eyes he loved. The eyes that always looked at him with such concern and care. They were clouded now, filled with uncertainty. He'd caused that. 'Bridie, I'm scared. Scared I'm going to get it wrong. Scared people will get ill. That they'll hate it. No,' he paused, 'they won't hate it. If I get it right, it'll be the best French dinner this festival has ever had.'

She reached out and placed her hands on his hips. His breath hitched. 'Can you please harness that confidence and believe in yourself. The beef is fresh, direct from a farm that I sourced myself. The chicken the same. This isn't seafood. This is good quality Australian farm-grown produce. You cannot go wrong.' Her breath brushed his cheek, and his knees went a little weak. 'I'm sorry for what I said earlier, I believe in you.'

'Please don't apologise. I stuffed-up. But I'm going to make it up to you with this dinner. Okay?'

'Don't do it for me, Caleb prove it to yourself.'

Their bodies touched. Her chest heaved and his mouth

went drier, if that was possible. Her stare contained longing and he matched her desire.

'I'm back!' Sybella came to stand between them.

His heart jolted. 'Hey, jitterbug.'

'Thank you, sweetie. Okay, Caleb. Take these.' Bridie punched out two strong painkillers and handed them over with more bottles of water. Then she mixed a Berocca and forced him to drink while the bubbles still fizzed.

'Now I'll be needing the toilet,' he groaned and Sybella laughed. 'Can always rely on you to laugh, hey,' he brushed his fingers over her cheek, and she asked him to lift her onto the bench.

'Uncle Caleb, do you think mummy would have liked the festival?'

The world around him stopped. 'She would have loved this festival, right? She wouldn't have had to do any cooking and there's music and dancing and games and rides. She would have taken you on the rides and…'

'Do you want to go on the rides with me?' Bridie interrupted.

Sybella declined. 'I want to stay here and help. I want to be a good cook.'

'Okay, Sybella, sweetie, I'd love your help. We have a lot of work to do, though, are you sure? You could be out having fun.'

'Yes, I want to help.'

'Okay, you help but Bridie has to go.'

'What? No, I'll help too.'

'No, I insist, you must go and reward yourself with the

spoils of your hard work.' Together big and little hands gently pushed her out of the tent.

'Okay, kiddo, let's do this.'

* * *

CALEB STOOD IN THE SHADOWS WATCHING THE CROWD. IT WAS A scene of pure joy: laughter, happy screams, people milling on picnic blankets and couples strolling hand in hand. In the dinner marquee guests finished off the last course. French cheeses were always something to linger over.

He was no festival connoisseur, but he gauged the event a huge success.

His head no longer throbbed, but his arms and legs ached, and his eyes were like saw-dust. In usual circumstances he'd pour another long-deserved drink after a frantic night in the kitchen. He realised with dawning clarity, that his behaviour had to change. Alcohol was to be enjoyed and fine wine an indulgence, not a coping mechanism to get through, get on and ultimately get out. He was a chef for goodness sake, he understood appreciating quality. Alcohol needed to be treated the same way.

And tonight, he'd cooked for one hundred people without a drop of alcohol in his system, well, none that wasn't left-over anyways. Triumphant! The first step in the right direction.

'Caleb, thank you, that was incredible,' Yvette patted him on the arm. 'The best meal I've had in a long time and certainly the best French festival.'

'That was awesome, man,' another bloke slapped him on the back as he exited the tent.

'Caleb,' Jacqueline paused for effect, touched him on the arm, 'that was amazing. You're an incredible chef, those flavours, the presentation, it was all sublime. In case you're unsure, you have a place in this town, you've earned it. I hope you'll stay.' That made his heart twist in his chest.

A procession of people left the marquee and each congratulated him. Could he accept that he might be back? That he'd overcome his disaster, his fear?

There was a heavier slap to his back and a hand gripping his.

'Good to see you.'

'Marco, you're here.'

'Had to come and check out where you've been hiding.' Caleb went to interrupt but Marco stopped him. 'No, it's okay. I understand. This place has potential, especially with this weird French thing it's got going on. There're a few vacant spots in town. Want to try something different?'

'Are you serious? You're happy to take another risk on me?'

'Of course. You're one of Australia's best chefs. We have some stuff to sort out with Lavapond before we can start a new venture, but yes, I say we do it. You will draw the crowds no matter where the restaurant is.'

'Mate, I won't let you down.'

'You never have,' and he walked away, 'oh and well done with your Insta feed and those pics, people love them, keep it up!'

What? He snatched out his phone and caught a glimpse of an endless feed of food pics, but Bridie approached.

'You did it.' She glowed in the moon-lit sky.

'You don't ever drink. You had some champagne today?'

'No, I don't usually drink. My father deals with life by drowning himself to the point he can't wake up the next day, and sometimes worse. I've detested drinking ever since, seen it as a sign of weakness, blamed it for making people behave badly, but it wasn't the drink, it was them. My father struggles and will probably always struggle, with or without alcohol. He has good and bad days. Like everyone else, I've indulged him and picked up the slack too often.'

'I'm so sorry about this morning. I'm not like your dad, I only ever used to drink in the kitchen, and it was a habit, not an addiction. Busy service, pressure, everyone did it. I realise it's a mistake and I promise to stop doing that.'

'For me?' her voice quavered.

'Yes, for you. I don't want to do anything that makes you uncomfortable.'

'Thank you,' she bowed her head before gazing into the distance. 'But I have to thank you too. You've made me realise that I'm not the one running this town, I am not the sole person responsible for the tuckshop, minding sick children, making cakes and running a farm and trying to translate books. I've always been alone and it's nice to be needed but it's become a bit out of hand.'

'A bit?' he joked. 'You won't have time to help others anyway because I need you. Sybella needs you.' He moved closer so his breath fanned her face, placed one hand to her cheek and let the other wind through her hair that flowed around her shoulders. Her eyelashes fluttered and she inched closer, their bodies warm. His head was pounding for a different reason as he massaged her cheek with his thumb and shivers of delight bolted through his body. He swept her hair to the side and planted a kiss to the soft skin of her neck. She leaned her head back in response and he trailed a row of kisses from her collar bone to her jaw. Their lips met and lust engulfed him, desire rocking through him. Caleb wanted more and he pressed harder and tasted all of her, smothering her with his kisses. She quivered under his touch, and he moved back to let them both catch their breath, but Bridie found his lips once more, her arms surrounding his back until his body burned.

A crack blasted above their heads and the sky erupted in a kaleidoscope of colour. Bursts of fireworks in spirals of red, white and blue filled the sky, trails of smoke billowing after each explosion. Caleb lowered his gaze and saw the lights reflected and dancing in Bridie's expression.

'Fireworks!' Came a shriek and little hands clasped around their joined legs. Caleb lifted Sybella up to join in their embrace and the three of them cuddled, enjoying the best French festival Bellethorpe had ever seen.

THE END

ABOUT THE AUTHOR

Leanne Lovegrove is a lawyer, wife and mother and a lover of romance and reading. Her law career created an addiction to coffee but provides countless story ideas. She is the author of five romance novels, and this is her third novella and second anthology. Leanne writes sweeping love stories with happily-ever-afters with strong female heroines and set in the beautiful landscape of Australia. She lives in Brisbane, Australia with her husband and three children.

To find out more about Leanne's books, you can find her here:

Web: www.leannelovegroveauthor.com

FaceBook: https://www.facebook.com/leannelovegroveauthor

Instagram: https://www.instagram.com/leannelovegroveauthor/

Bookbub: https://www.bookbub.com/profile/leanne-lovegrove

How far would you go to save your family home?

Her Outback Home

LEANNE LOVEGROVE

HER OUTBACK HOME

Here's what reviewers are saying about Leanne's latest release:

A well written gripping read. The characters were charismatic, authentic and well executed. I especially liked the character of Hannah and her commitment, devotion and endurance towards her family and life – Bianca Mal, reviewer_(Instagram)

Well written and loved it immensely – Nicole, reviewer, Goodreads

Her Outback home is a captivating, emotional and inspiring story of love, family and the world around us. What a fantastic read – chapter_ichi, book reviewer, Instagram / Goodreads.

A heartwarming story of respect and love for family and the environment we live in – ms.gsbookshelf – Instagram

Leanne has a fine way of creating such likeable character and touching on so many deep and important topics. I love the way Leanne brought so many important topics together in this story. I love the setting and I was drawn in from the very first page. A beautifully written and captivating story – allbookedout_with-mj – Instagram

Link: mybook.to / outbackhome

Leanne's other novels:

Unexpected Delivery

mybook.to / unexpectedelivery

Illegal Love

mybook.to / illegallove

Keeper of the Light

mybook.to/KeeperoftheLight

A Good Life

mybook.to/AGoodLife

Novellas:

Escapades of a Personal Stylist

mybook.to/escapades

Love on the Sweeping Plains

mybook.to/SweepingPlains

Anthologies:

Love in a Sunburnt Land

getbook.at/SunburntLand

Love in a Sunburnt Land volume 2

getbook.at/SunburntLand2